HAPPIER
SHE'S EV

HAPPIER THAN SHE'S EVER BEEN...

MENNA VAN PRAAG

HAY HOUSE

Australia • Canada • Hong Kong • India
South Africa • United Kingdom • United States

First published and distributed in the United Kingdom by:
Hay House UK Ltd, 292B Kensal Rd, London W10 5BE.
Tel.: (44) 20 8962 1230; Fax: (44) 20 8962 1239. www.hayhouse.co.uk

Published and distributed in the United States of America by:
Hay House, Inc., PO Box 5100, Carlsbad, CA 92018-5100.
Tel.: (1) 760 431 7695 or (800) 654 5126; Fax: (1) 760 431 6948 or (800) 650 5115.
www.hayhouse.com

Published and distributed in Australia by:
Hay House Australia Ltd, 18/36 Ralph St, Alexandria NSW 2015.
Tel.: (61) 2 9669 4299; Fax: (61) 2 9669 4144. www.hayhouse.com.au

Published and distributed in the Republic of South Africa by:
Hay House SA (Pty), Ltd, PO Box 990, Witkoppen 2068.
Tel./Fax: (27) 11 467 8904. www.hayhouse.co.za

Published and distributed in India by:
Hay House Publishers India, Muskaan Complex, Plot No.3, B-2, Vasant Kunj,
New Delhi – 110 070. Tel.: (91) 11 4176 1620; Fax: (91) 11 4176 1630.
www.hayhouse.co.in

Distributed in Canada by:
Raincoast, 9050 Shaughnessy St, Vancouver, BC V6P 6E5.
Tel.: (1) 604 323 7100; Fax: (1) 604 323 2600

© Menna van Praag, 2011

A catalogue record for this book is available from the British Library.

ISBN 978-1-84850-213-0

Printed and bound in Great Britain by
TJ International, Padstow, Cornwall.

For Ariel & Shya

*– who inspire me to create my own
magical relationship every day –*

with love

Fairy Tales

May Fitzgerald was happy. Happier than she'd ever been in her life. All her dreams had finally fallen into place. After many years of striving and suffering, disappointments and despair, misery and mistakes, and after many life lessons, everything had at last come together. Now she lived in a beautiful city, in a beautiful home, with the most beautiful man she'd ever met. And her book – the one she'd needed so much courage to create, the one she'd sold her café to self-publish, the one she'd travelled across America to sell – was steadily becoming rather successful.

May had also stopped stuffing herself with vast quantities of chocolate to suppress her sadness. Which was easy, since she wasn't sad any more.

So she could leave chocolate bars in the fridge for weeks on end without being remotely tempted to scoff them all at once.

May was extremely grateful for her new life. She thought often about her old one and how she might never have found the courage to leave it if not for the help she'd received from all the magical people she'd met. Most especially Rose, the little old lady with the sparkling blue eyes, who had found May full of loneliness and self-loathing in her café. And Faith, her cousin and the loveliest friend one could ever hope to have. Without them May would still be sitting behind the counter at The Cocoa Café, sobbing into her cappuccinos, gobbling entire cakes and falling in love with men who didn't want her.

Yet because of them here she was in America, living all her dreams at once. Even after a year, May could still hardly believe it was true and regularly had to pinch herself just to be sure she was awake. Now May dedicated her free time to helping other women who were suffering with the same issues she'd struggled with for so long. Since they might not be lucky enough to meet inspirational people by chance, and certainly wouldn't bump into Rose in their local café, May hoped to be the magical stranger in their lives, the one who set them on the path to their own particular joys. And when these women came back to tell her how much she'd helped them and how much happier they were now, May felt more joyful and grateful than she'd ever imagined possible.

Every Tuesday and Thursday evening at her boyfriend Ben's bookshop May held special open events. She baked a few goodies for those who came, read passages from her book, answered questions, played games and generally did whatever she could to bring a little joy into their lives and, hopefully, some long-term happiness too. One day, as she was clearing up after a particularly wonderful evening, May remembered something the lovely Rose had said to her: that she mustn't feel guilty about being happy, because people who are happy spread their joy, sprinkling it all over the people they meet, while unhappy people do just the opposite. So being happy was really about being a bright light in a dark world. Which was exactly what May wanted to be.

Every day for the past few months May had awoken to sunlight streaming through her windows, such were the benefits of a San Franciscan summer, and every day she lay under the duvet for a little while, just smiling to herself. No matter where she was in the world, or what she was doing, May always woke up early. Having run a café for a decade, the instinct was now embedded in her. But she didn't mind. In fact she loved having time to let the sunlight sink into her skin, to strengthen and fortify herself, before the day really began.

When May got up she left Ben snoring softly beside her and padded over to the kitchen in her pyjamas. They lived in a little two-storey flat above his bookshop, left to him by his grandfather. It had been the first ever bookshop to stock May's novel and to honour it with a window display. Living above about two thousand books thrilled May more than she could possibly put into words. Sometimes, very early in the morning, she'd tiptoe down the little spiral staircase and just stand on the bottom step, gazing out at the maze of bookshelves that were weighed down to breaking point, then up at the golden stars that studded the deep-blue ceiling, and down at the oak floors. And, as she breathed in the slightly musty smell, May would let out a small sigh of pure gratitude.

Her life with Ben was a simple one, and she absolutely adored it. Not having much money, their evenings alternated between going for walks in the city and visiting their favourite free haunts: the Japanese Tea Garden, the bench on a hill overlooking the Golden Gate Bridge, window shopping on Height Street, sharing coffee and cake at The Tea Cup. When the bookshop closed they spent hours exploring, reading each other passages from their best-loved books and making love in every aisle. Upstairs in the flat, when they weren't in bed they were in the kitchen. Ben did most of the cooking, while May did most of the eating and post-prandial cleaning.

Of course, amid all this bountiful joy, they still had disagreements, even the occasional fight. They had bad days and sometimes took out their hurt and frustration on each other, but they were never calculating or cruel; they merely made surface scratches, easily rubbed off, that never undermined the safety they felt together.

For the first few months May had felt nervous, remembering how her last heart-breaking relationship flew for a few blissful months, then quickly crashed and burned. So she was always a little anxious, waiting for the day Ben would tell her he didn't love her any more. But then months passed, then nearly a year, and nothing changed. He still loved and wanted her just as much as she loved and wanted him. And that was such a blessing May still couldn't quite believe it. When she'd fallen for the stunning, emotionally unobtainable Jake, who was driven away by her neediness and neuroses, May had thought she was doomed, that she'd have to resign herself to a life without love. And, miracle of miracles, now it seemed she'd met her soulmate.

Every morning she made fresh coffee, which she took to Ben, who couldn't function before his first gulps of caffeine. On Saturdays and Sundays she made blueberry scones. Now that she no longer *had* to bake dozens of cakes each morning, May rather enjoyed creating delicious treats in their tiny kitchen and filling the flat with the smells of cinnamon buns, chocolate tarts, lavender doughnuts, vanilla macaroons… Sadly she had tried in vain to find all the ingredients for chocolate flapjacks in the shops she'd visited (and had been surprised to discover that, across the pond, flapjacks were actually a type of pancake) so Ben had yet to taste her speciality. But the week before, on the anniversary of her mother's birth, May had made Lily's favourite rosewater and white chocolate cake, and Ben had declared it the best thing he'd ever eaten in his life. Ever. And then she'd showered him with kisses.

After Ben had sipped his coffee and snuggled with May until he was almost late, then dragged himself out of bed, showered and taken a second cup to his desk downstairs in the bookshop, May would trot up another spiral staircase in her pyjamas and sink into the sofa of the little room that was hers alone. A week after she'd moved into Ben's flat, only three weeks after they'd actually met, he'd created a special space just for her: to write, to think, to be.

It was a small room. One wall was a large window overlooking a long street that dipped down towards the sea and was lined on either side with different coloured houses. In the distance, on a clear day, the red railings of the famous bridge were just visible. May loved to stare out of that window. For weeks now she hadn't written a single word but had simply gazed and smiled up at the sky. She felt a new kind of happiness: one that wanted nothing, needed nothing and knew that everything was absolutely perfect, just the way it was. In this mood, May found it impossible to pick up her pen, because nothing else needed to be said.

So instead she doodled. Drawing patterns and random words in large elaborate letters, the long thin curl of consonants and vowels reaching up and gliding down the page. Sometimes it felt as though she was waiting. She sensed that her next story was inside her, slowly forming, and she just had to pass the time until it was ready to be born. And May was quite happy to wait; she was no longer frantic or scared of the failure to succeed, the inability to achieve anything. She felt complete. Just as she was. She didn't need to be special, or to produce something spectacular, in order to be a better person. She knew that nothing she did could add to or take away from the simple perfection of exactly who she was, from the tips of her fingers to the depths of her heart.

As a child and a teenager, in fact up until a year ago, May had felt unlovable. And, looking back on it, she knew it had started when she was six years old, when her father had left. Although her mother had told her over and over again that it wasn't her fault, that he still loved her, May had never believed it. She worried there was something really wrong with her; she feared a secret reason too horrible for her mother to express. Over the years the reason took various forms: she was too ugly, too boring, too stupid, too plain, too simple, too... And when her father never came back, she knew they must *all* be true. She'd taken these insecurities into every short-lived relationship she'd ever had. In the beginning May had always feared she'd be abandoned once they decided she was too fat and discovered all her other imperfections. And so, despite her best efforts to the contrary, she became needy and clingy, and leave her they always did, confirming all her worst fears about how unlovable she really was.

At a young age, to try to do something special, she'd started to write. And ever since May had finished her first story and her teacher displayed it on the wall, she'd dreamed of getting a real novel published: one that would lead to great acclaim, fame and fortune. Then her father would one day see it in a bookshop window. He'd buy it, adore it, read all the reviews; he'd see how everyone else loved her. And he'd realise what an awful mistake he'd made, what a horror he'd been; then he'd drop everything and dedicate his days to finding her again.

Of course now that she'd self-published her book, and it was selling only in San Francisco and hadn't had a single review, good or bad, all those hopes about her father seemed very unlikely. But luckily she didn't feel the pain of his leaving as sharply any more. It had used to feel like a red-hot poker, branding lovelessness across her heart. And when Jake left her the sense of lovelessness scarred May deeper still. However, now with the certainty of Ben's love and, more importantly, her own, her father's absence had become an occasional cold breath that blew across her face.

Today May sat at her desk, legs crossed on her red leather chair. She chewed the end of her pen absently and gazed out of the window. Just then, a big fluffy ball of fur tumbled onto the desk, having jumped rather haphazardly from the top of a nearby bookshelf. It was Doughnut, her cat.

'Hey, my gorgeous ball of nuttiness.' May smiled, running her fingers through his long grey-and-white fur. Doughnut purred loudly and pressed his head into the palm of her hand. She scratched his ears and he began drooling. May laughed.

She'd been back to England a few months earlier to renew her visa again, visit her wonderful cousin, Faith, and finally collect Doughnut, who she'd left in Faith's safekeeping. She'd also visited her mother's grave, placing a fresh rosewater and white chocolate cake by the headstone, as was her tradition, and smiling to see her again. May hadn't stayed in England long, and she hadn't been very sad to leave. Although she missed Faith, being an insular, introverted loner during her life in England, May hadn't made any other friends – with the exception of her ex-boyfriend Jake. And, given the heart-shattering disaster that had been, she hoped never to see *him* again. Nevertheless it was still a shock, given how scared she'd been to come to America, to realise how much like home this new country now felt.

Of all the places she'd been in America, and admittedly it wasn't many, San Francisco was the one she'd immediately fallen in love with. The place she'd known was hers. And so it was. A reward, a gift, after all those painful, lonely years of struggling so hard to become the woman she'd always wanted to be, San Francisco was her homecoming.

May stroked Doughnut, gazed out of the window and realised that no words were coming to her today. She would have to wait. In the past, when she had striven to achieve something, to justify her place in the world and prove herself worthy of love, May had found waiting for results absolutely agonising. But now she didn't mind at all.

'Come on, you big beautiful ball of fluff.' May picked up the cat and carried him, floppy and content, down the short spiral staircase. 'I know it's not Sunday, but I think it's a good time for blueberry scones, don't you?' Doughnut purred.

May loved Ben's kitchen. She loved the wooden doors of the cabinets, each painted a different colour: egg-yolk yellow, sea blue, blood red, leaf green. She loved the gas cooker and the cast-iron saucepans, the old oak chopping boards, the fifties-style heavy ceramic cream mixing bowls with blue trim. And she loved baking in it.

A few times a week, in addition to her own *Men, Money and Chocolate* evenings, May resurrected The Cocoa Café in that kitchen and created treats for Ben's bookshop events: talks by his favourite authors, or random readings of his favourite books. At the first one that May had attended, there were thirty kids, all under the age of ten. They'd been running around the bookshop, squealing up and down the aisles, terrifying May until she scurried into the Magical Realism section and hid inside a signed first edition of *Like Water for Chocolate*. But when Ben began reading from *Alice Through the Looking Glass* the children all flopped onto the floor and gazed up at him, rapt and immobile until, an hour later, he closed the book, promising to return with them to Wonderland next week. May had been enthralled along with them. Ben was the most captivating reader she'd ever heard and, watching how much he loved the story and how he cared about those children, May realised she wanted to spend the rest of her life with him.

This evening marked his monthly gathering of sci-fi geeks. They had proclaimed this the year of Neil Gaiman and were steadily working their way through each of his fantasy novels. May wasn't a fan of science fiction, so she left them to it, but had promised Ben that tonight she'd provide them all with sugary sustenance to see them through the opening chapters of *Stardust*. So she set to work.

An hour later, just before lunchtime, May descended the main spiral staircase to Ben's bookshop. Before his grandfather had converted it, the building had been a fire station and the staircase had replaced the emergency pole. Doughnut padded down the steps and followed May to Ben's desk, where he was hidden behind several boxes of second-hand books. He looked up as May approached.

'Hey, beautiful.'

'Hey, sexy, need any help?'

'That'd be great.' Ben smiled. 'Can you start early?'

'Sure.' May nodded. Every afternoon she worked in the bookshop so Ben could visit buyers, do his accounts and run various errands.

He stopped unpacking books and held her gaze. 'Still no words?'

May shook her head but smiled at him, happy that he knew her so well and cared so much.

'They'll come back,' Ben said. 'Don't worry.'

'I know they will,' May said, nodding. 'I just miss them a little, that's all.'

Ben stepped round the desk and pulled his girlfriend into a hug. She pressed her face against his chest, breathing him in. Doughnut wound round their legs, squeezing figures-of-eight between them.

May looked up at Ben. 'I've made four batches of blueberry scones.'

'That's wonderful,' he said, grinning. 'The geeks will really appreciate them.'

'Off you go then,' May said. 'Go and do whatever it is you must do. I'll take care of everything here.'

'Thank you.' Ben kissed her, grabbed a box off the desk and almost tripped over Doughnut as he hurried down an aisle of books towards the door.

That evening May leant against a bookshelf, watching Ben weaving between his sci-fi geeks, a plate of her blueberry scones in his hand. He was smiling at everyone, touching the shy people's shoulders to put them at ease, looking them in the eye, holding their gaze, listening so they felt like the only person in the room. How was it possible to love another human being this much? May sighed happily. Instantly a familiar fear rose up inside her: that it wouldn't last, that it'd all be taken away again, that she'd lose everything, even herself. This was the only thing that still troubled her, this fear. It caught her off guard, usually just after her happiest moments, and she didn't know what to do with it. She didn't want to talk about it, in case that only made it worse, nor did she want to think too much or over-analyse it. So instead she suppressed it, and picked up another plate of scones.

DREAMS

Two weeks later May awoke in the middle of the night, her heart beating so fast she could hardly breathe. She glanced over at Ben sleeping next to her softly emitting little snores, put her hand on his bare shoulder and held it there. The touch steadied her, anchoring her in reality: Ben beside her and Doughnut snuggled in the folds of bright blue blankets, a big fluffy ball in a sea of sheets.

Gradually, as the minutes ticked by, May's breathing steadied and she sank back into her pillows with a sigh. She stared up at the patches of moonlight shimmering across the ceiling, trying to remember her nightmare. May glanced at the alarm clock – three thirty-three a.m. – and smiled slightly. Thirty-three: her lucky number, her birth number. Perhaps that was a good sign. Everything was fine. It was just a bad dream, nothing more. She was safe. And happy. And fine. Fine. Fine. Fine. May tucked her hands under the covers as Ben rolled over onto his stomach. She pressed her right palm against his bare back, closed her eyes and refused to admit she was slightly too scared to go back to sleep.

The next afternoon May reshelved the Science Fiction & Fantasy section. It was a quiet day. By teatime she'd sold a total of three books on Astrology and one Harry Potter book that Ben kept in the section on Witchcraft for Kids: Fiction. As May worked, slotting the books into alphabetical order, she started to remember last night. Single words and snapshot images floated into her mind, slowly settling into her consciousness like snowfall.

Fantasy. A woman's smile. Fairy tales. A string of pearls. Smiling eyes. Wrinkled skin. True love. Safety. Sitting on her daddy's lap. Snuggled in Ben's arms. Joy. Coming home.

Holding a copy of *Coraline* in one hand, May stopped for a moment. Perhaps the dream had been a happy one. She'd been worrying about nothing. It was fine. Everything was fine. May turned back to the shelf, then stopped, holding the book in mid-air.

False love. Fear. Panic. Anger. Despair. Reality. A scream, her scream. Feet running, dashing through a forest, faster and faster. Lies. Her heart beating in her mouth. Ba-bum, ba-bum, ba-bum. Louder and louder. Fear. Loss. Her feet tripping on a log, falling into a deep, never-ending black hole. Falling and falling and falling into…

May dropped the book to the floor.

Distracting herself with a few more sales and spending half an hour chatting with a customer about their favourite Alice Hoffman books, May got through the rest of the day without thinking about the dream again. Or, at least, not every other second. When she went upstairs that evening Ben had made sea bass in white wine and butter sauce, with curly kale and purple sprouting broccoli for dinner. Her favourite.

'Are you okay, *bichana*?' Ben asked, as they sat on the floor, their plates on the coffee table. It was his pet name for her, meaning 'kitten' in Portuguese. And it was what his mother had called him as a child, though of course using the male form: *bichano*. Sometimes, when she was feeling adventurous, May used it too.

'Yeah.' May glanced up. 'I… it, um, well, it was just a slow day, that's all. I don't like them so much, they make me worry.'

'Don't worry,' Ben said, smiling. 'We'll be okay. It will all even out in the end, good days and bad; it always does.'

'Yeah, I suppose so,' May said. 'You know, I should have had that attitude when I was running The Cocoa Café, then maybe I wouldn't have lost everything.'

'Perhaps,' Ben said, 'but then you'd never have published your book or crossed the ocean and I'd never have met you. Which would have been a very bad thing indeed.'

'That's true.' May smiled. 'It's like Shakespeare wrote: "*There is nothing either good or bad, but thinking makes it so.*" I suppose that's true. Though it's sometimes hard to think so when you're in the middle of some messy, totally tragic event.' The first one that came to May's mind was the humiliating and heart-crushing break-up with Jake, the only man she thought she'd been so in love with before Ben. The one who'd taken her right to the edge of sanity and self-loathing. But of course she couldn't mention that now.

'Hey.' Ben reached over the plates to take May's hand across the table. 'You seem a little sad. What's up?'

May shrugged, thinking it was too silly to talk about. 'Nothing, it's nothing, I don't know.'

'You do,' he said, 'I think you do.'

'No, it's nothing,' May said. 'It's silly.'

'Tell me.'

'I had this dream last night. I couldn't sleep afterwards. And, I don't know, I haven't been able to stop thinking about it.'

'Oh.' Ben squeezed May's hand. A little rush of warmth flooded her body, and she felt again how lucky she was to be loved by this man. 'So, what was the dream about?'

May glanced down at the last piece of broccoli on her plate. She prodded it with her fork. 'I don't know,' she lied, scared to bring up the subject. 'I can't remember.'

That night Ben didn't fall asleep as quickly as usual. He knew May wasn't telling him the truth. At least not entirely. And it worried him that she would retreat into herself when he was right next to her and wanting to help. But he didn't press her, thinking it best to let May tell him in her own time. He turned his head to see the luminous red lights of the alarm clock: twelve twenty-one. Past midnight. The eighth of October. Two weeks until the anniversary of their first kiss. And tonight was the first time they'd turned out the lights without making love. May had her eyes closed, but Ben knew she wasn't asleep. He felt a tiny distance springing up between them, something he'd never felt before. He reached out to gently stroke May's long, thick, dark hair. But the space was still there. Eventually, not knowing what else to do, Ben finally closed his eyes and let himself fall asleep.

As soon as she heard Ben's breathing deepen and slow, May opened her eyes. She still felt the small stabs of guilt in her chest for not telling him the truth. But she hadn't wanted to bring up the pain of her past, hadn't wanted to create a problem, to create concern where perhaps there was none. For the past year everything had been, for the first time in May's life, so perfect. And she couldn't bear to spoil it, especially with the fragments of fantasies. It was nearly four o'clock before May finally drifted to sleep. And, almost as soon as she did, she began to dream.

She was in a field full of daisies and daffodils and apple trees in blossom. A gentle breeze blew around her and pinkish petals drifted through the air, floating into her palms as she reached out to touch them. Then suddenly, as her fingers closed around the blossom, everything vanished and she was left standing on a wasteland. The ground was barren and bare, with tufts of dry grass scattered across the empty field. A few trees remained, stripped down, their skeleton fingers grasping at the wind.

May felt a knot of fear twisting in her throat. She looked out to the horizon to see a figure walking slowly towards her and, before she could see more than an outline, before the figure was anything other than a shadow, May knew who it was.

'Rose,' May whispered, as the woman reached her, looking exactly as she remembered: thin and tiny, dressed in a twin set and pearls, with those little sparkling blue eyes and an enormous smile on her lips. May thought of the café, the chocolate flapjacks, meeting this old woman who'd touched her heart and saved her life, and the memory shone bright in her heart as though it was yesterday.

'I knew it was you,' May said softly. 'I hoped…'

'Did you?' The old lady smiled. 'So why the desolate landscape, my dear?' She threw a tiny birdlike hand in the direction of the wasteland. 'Why ever would you conjure up this?'

'I suppose I was scared.'

'Of what, my dear?'

'I don't know,' May admitted.

'Well, enough of that,' Rose said. 'Let's brighten this dream up a bit.'

And, with that, she snapped her tiny fingers. Instantly the landscape disappeared and they were sitting back in The Cocoa Café, the place they'd met over two years ago, at the table where they'd sat and talked, and May's life had changed forever.

'A reunion.' May smiled. 'It's a shame we can't eat flapjacks too. I haven't had them in so long.'

'We can eat whatever you want, my dear,' Rose said, laughing, the sound tinkling through the air. 'This is your dream, after all.' She clicked her fingers again and a plate piled high with chocolate flapjacks appeared on the table. May grinned and two steaming mugs of hot chocolate materialised into their hands.

'Perfect.' May sighed happily.

'Perfect,' Rose echoed, 'and, funnily enough, that's exactly the topic I came to talk to you about, before it's too late.'

'Too late for what?' May asked, suddenly anxious. 'What's wrong? I thought everything was okay now. I took all your advice last time. I was courageous and compassionate. I came here; I sold my books; I met Ben. I'm not a miserable thing any more. I'm helping people; I'm being a bright light in a dark world, just like you said. I'm no longer drowning my sorrow in vats of chocolate, and I haven't given up my life and my sense of self for a man, not since that disaster with Jake when I became all needy and clingy and let my world revolve around him until he ran away screaming… Well, I – I thought everything was just perfect now. I thought I'd got it right this time.'

'Oh, don't worry so much, dear,' Rose said, patting May's hand with her tiny wrinkled fingers. 'There's nothing very wrong yet, and there needn't be anything wrong, so long as you don't get attached to the idea of perfection.'

'What?' May frowned, thoroughly confused.

'You have the idea, my dear, that when you find the right relationship it will be "perfect". But this is not true, at least not in the way you think of perfection – as a life together without upset or upheaval, where you always agree, see life in the same way and want the same things –'

'But… but,' May stumbled, 'we do – we are. That's what it's like with Ben. That's how I know he's my soulmate.'

'Oh, my dear.' Rose sighed and sipped her hot chocolate. 'I'm sorry to burst your bubble, but a soulmate isn't what you think it is.'

'What?' May asked, feeling anxiety rising in her throat. 'What do you mean?'

'Well, my dear,' Rose said gently, 'like most people on the planet, you have a rather highly polished view of love: romance, sunsets, long walks on the beach and all that. You think that once you meet "the one" everything will fall into place. You'll match perfectly. You'll never disagree, fight, feel attracted to other people, get angry or want to hurt each other. You think that being soulmates means a total absence of pain, conflict, anger and fear.'

'Well, doesn't it?' May frowned again.

'No.' Rose nibbled a chocolate flapjack. 'A soulmate is not someone who never challenges you, always agrees with you and sees everything exactly the way you see it. A soulmate is someone who helps you to grow, to have courage when you're scared, to forgive, to see another point of view; someone who will be gentle with you, and honest, a mirror that won't hurt you but will show you the truth. So you can learn both to love yourself the way you are and to be, at least most of the time, the happiest, kindest and most compassionate version of you. And so sometimes, when you lose your way, he'll challenge you. If you get caught up in the trap of money and fame, striving for things that you think will bring you happiness, he'll remind you –'

'Are you saying that's what I'm going to do?' May asked. 'Because I don't think so. I think I've learnt all my life lessons now. I think it's all going to be fine. I've been through the pain, I've got it all worked out.'

'Oh, my dear!' Rose laughed. 'The minute you think *that*, you're in trouble. Life is always changing, always throwing up new lessons to learn; you're going to be reacting and responding to things, for better or worse, until you die. You're not a monk sitting on a mountain top; you're a real woman trying to do the best you can in an often crazy world. Some days you'll be happy and centred and kind; other times you'll be fearful and lost and do or say something you regret. I'm afraid it's never over, it never stops.'

'Oh dear.' May sighed. 'Oh dear, I thought…'

'But you don't have to worry, my love,' Rose said. 'Remember to always have compassion for yourself and everyone else learning their lessons around you; then you'll be okay, no matter what.'

'I don't understand though,' May said. 'If a soulmate brings you as much pain as any other relationship, then what's the point? What's the point of finding someone you really love? You might as well just settle for anyone.'

'Oh no,' Rose said, 'it's not the same at all. The gut-wrenching pain of being with the wrong person feels entirely different from the growing pains of being with your soulmate. Don't worry. It won't be the same with Ben as it was with Jake, not at all.'

May breathed a sigh of relief and reached for a flapjack. 'Well, that's good, because I don't know if my heart could take that kind of pain again.'

'But you still have to be prepared for the growing pains, the life lessons you'll go through together,' Rose said. 'You can't avoid them. So don't resist the more difficult things that happen. Because if you try to stick your head in the sand, it'll only make it more painful in the end.'

'So,' May asked, 'how do I not do that?'

'Be honest,' Rose said firmly. 'Last night you lied to him. You tried to pretend that everything was fine because you wanted it to be. But when you're not honest about the way you really feel, no matter how scary that is, then slowly but surely you'll lose touch with your heart and with your true love.'

'I don't know if I can,' May said. 'I don't know if I have the courage for this.'

'Oh, my dear.' Rose patted her hand again. 'Of course you do. And, if you let him, Ben will be right there with you. You've had the honeymoon stage to help cement you together. Now it's time for the next stage: going through the fire of self-discovery, seeing each other for how you truly are, with all your unresolved issues, angers and upsets. These have been hidden under the first glow of false love, but they'll pop up soon enough. They have to so that you can complete all the unresolved pains you carry within you.'

May frowned. 'Like what?'

'Well, your secret fears that you really are unlovable,' Rose said, 'that you'll be abandoned, that all men will eventually leave you like your father did.'

'B-but,' May stuttered, 'I thought… I thought –'

'That you had already resolved that?' Rose smiled.

'Well, yes,' May admitted. 'I suppose so.'

'There are many layers to your self, many lessons in life you don't yet know,' Rose said, 'so remember: don't get too attached to the idea of a life without challenges and upheavals. Or you'll have to pretend that everything is great even when it isn't, that you feel happy even when you don't. And *that*, my dear, is how you lose your heart.'

May looked at Rose, trying not to get too scared.

'And there will be moments to come,' Rose continued, 'and they will be painful if you resist them, if you believe that joy is better than sorrow, that painless is better than painful, that peace is better than anger, and calm better than upset… Because if you think that all the "good" ways of being are superior to the "bad", then you won't be able to be true to yourself or the way that you feel. Then you'll begin to pretend, fake and lie… you'll judge your partner for the "negative" in him, and you will withdraw. And, my dear, that will be the beginning of the end.'

By this time May was staring at Rose open-mouthed, having left her flapjack on the table, all thoughts of it forgotten. 'But I – I don't want to do that,' she stuttered. 'I don't want to lie, judge, withdraw and…'

'Well,' Rose said, 'then you must be willing to keep on walking, through the flower gardens and through the fire. Because you still have more wounds to heal within you, and Ben will help you bring them to the surface. He will tickle and tease you, and everything unresolved inside will come out. But if you don't want to feel it, if you want to deny any anger, pain, hatred within you, then his tickles will feel like punches and his teasing will feel like slaps.'

By now May had stood up and was pacing up and down the length of the little café, wringing her hands together. 'But this sounds awful, absolutely awful. I don't want to go through this, I really don't…'

'That's only your fear speaking, my dear,' Rose said calmly. 'If you stand strong in the middle of this circle of fire, you won't get burned, I promise you. But if you keep darting in and out, not trusting yourself or your lover, then it will hurt; it will brand you with scars that may take years to heal.'

May looked stricken and stopped walking.

'Don't worry, my dear, those scars always heal,' Rose said, smiling, 'if you can find the courage to remember that a true soulmate is not supposed to "complete" you but challenge you. With his actions and his being, he'll invite you to look at those things inside yourself that you may not want to see – but these aren't bad things, my dear, just behaviours and beliefs that may hurt before they are resolved. And if you allow this, it can be a beautiful process.'

'Really?' May asked.

'Yes, really,' Rose said, 'so long as you keep reaching for Ben's hand, especially in those moments when what you really want to do is slap him and run away. But if you blame him for what he sees and says, it'll easily be the most painful process you've ever been through. And if you try to run from it, then you might be running for the rest of your life.'

May stared at Rose with tears in her eyes.

'And every time you have the courage to stand strong in the face of your fears, to stay together and keep loving each other through the growing pains,' Rose told her, 'you'll be rewarded with the greatest gift of all.'

'What's that?' May asked.

'Well, the ultimate purpose of your soulmate,' Rose explained, 'is to give you the gift of unconditional love. Firstly by loving you before he really knows you, and then by loving you after he knows *everything*. Of course, he'll only be able to do that if you do it too. For it is one thing to love yourself when you're happy, peaceful, joyful and calm. It's quite another to still love yourself when you're sad, angry, upset and stressed. And you, my dear May, you still have this to learn. And, if you let him, Ben will help teach you how.' Rose smiled her most magnificent smile and her little blue eyes twinkled with compassion and love. And then she disappeared.

May awoke, her heart beating fast, palms sweating, her T-shirt sticking to her chest. She blinked in the darkness trying to catch her breath. She glanced over at Ben sleeping soundly, a little smile on his lips. In that moment May had the urge to cling to him and never let go. In the next, to leap out of bed, run and never look back. But instead she remained still, then slowly sank back into her pillow and stared up at the ceiling. For the next five hours, until the sun came up, May wondered over and over again whether or not, when the time came to it, she would have the courage to stand strong in the centre of the circle of fire or if she would get burned.

❀ ❀ ❀

FEAR

'Are you sure you're okay?' Ben asked, as May sat down on the edge of the bed and handed him his morning cup of coffee. He held her gaze as she looked at him. For a moment May almost said something, almost told him everything. But she was scared, of so many things. Of Ben thinking she was crazy, of creating conflict, of losing what they had together. So instead she shook her head.

'No, I'm fine,' May said, 'and I love you.'

'I love you too.' Ben kissed her, knowing something was up and hoping May would tell him when she was ready. He didn't want to press her, didn't want to push her away. So, in that moment, as they both suppressed their feelings instead of speaking up, their relationship was knocked a few degrees off course. But the shift was so subtle that neither of them even noticed what was happening.

That afternoon May cleaned. It was an old habit she had when she wasn't expressing herself, though she wasn't really aware of it. She set to work on the bookshop, hoovering the floors, dusting the shelves and rubbing the books' spines with a tea towel. She'd made it halfway along the third shelf of the Astrology, Astronomy & Alchemy section when Ben hurried in through the front door. May glanced up, feeling the now familiar surge of happiness she got whenever she saw him. Though this time she also felt a tiny undercurrent of trepidation. She should talk to him, tell the truth, be honest – just as Rose advised. And she would; she just didn't have the guts to do it quite yet. 'Hey, you're early.'

'The guy didn't show,' Ben said, referring to a source who sometimes supplied him with second-hand books. 'He gets good books, but he's a bit of a feckless bum.'

'Are you trying to be a Brit again?' May raised an eyebrow with a smile and walked towards him.

'Yep, I'm learning your ways,' Ben teased, 'the self-deprecating wit, the self-flagellating false modesty, the condescending sarcasm…'

'You forget our innate and effortless superiority,' May added, laughing, 'especially to all things American.'

'Oh, is that so?'

'But of course.' May smiled as he stepped close to her and slid a single finger down the front of her shirt, grazing the top of her breasts.

'Well then, I think it's time you taught me some of your superior skills,' Ben whispered into her neck. 'I might still have a lot to learn.'

'Yes, you might,' May breathed as his tongue followed his fingers. 'Oh, Ben, no, not here. We might scandalise a young child, scar it for life.'

'Oh, yes?' Ben gave her an impish grin. 'Why – are we going to be very naughty?'

'Not here, we're not,' May said in teacherish tones.

'Okay then.' Ben leapt over to the door, turned the lock and the 'Closed' sign over, rushed back and grabbed May's hand. 'I think it's time to go upstairs.'

'Okay,' she giggled, wondering if it was possible to love someone more than she loved Ben.

They lay together in bed, the late afternoon sun falling through the windows and warming their bare skin. Words danced around May's mind, forming and reforming, trying to explain something she didn't quite comprehend, to describe a feeling she'd never felt before, to articulate a fear she couldn't put her finger on. But everything between them still felt so nearly perfect that it seemed silly to upset it for the sake of something half-imagined and half-understood.

As he looked at her Ben knew this was the moment to ask May what was wrong. And May knew it was the moment to tell him. But both were too scared to cause cracks in the closeness they'd so carefully and lovingly created.

'I love you,' she said.

'I love you too,' he said.

Afterwards they dressed, had dinner, then watched a TV show to distract them from the silence and separation that was, by now, just a little bigger, just a few inches wider, than before.

May took the next day off from the bookshop and, leaving Ben painting the walls of the Magical Mystery section bright yellow, set off downtown to give a book reading in a little café. The owner, a regular customer of Ben's, had invited May along to entertain her customers one afternoon and May, extremely flattered at the offer, had said yes.

The Tea Cup was a sweet coffee shop that reminded May a little of The Cocoa Café. Light pink-and-white-striped wallpaper lined the walls, and creamy soft sofas and chairs were scattered across fluffy carpets. It was, May thought, rather like walking into a bowl of multicoloured marshmallows, and she loved it.

The first time May had done a book reading at Ben's bookshop – suggested and organised by him – she'd been dragged to it kicking and screaming. Not literally, but almost. Although May had really wanted to connect with other women, to tell them about her experiences, about what she learnt about life, love and weight-loss, and to help them if she could, she'd also been terrified that no one would show up, or only one person would, thus making her humiliation public, or that many people would arrive but they'd all hate it and boo her off. As it was, seven women came along, each clutching a copy of *Men, Money and Chocolate*, and they'd listened closely while she talked about her life, asked May for advice on theirs and clapped with great enthusiasm at the end. When she saw their faces at the end, full of renewed hope for love and excitement for life, May was absolutely touched and delighted. She'd found her calling, her way to give back to world, to say thank you for everything she'd been given.

Today about thirty people came, filling the little café to the brim. They crowded onto the sofas and comfy chairs and even spilled onto the carpets. They were all drinking coffee, eating cake and holding her book in their hands.

'Hello, welcome.' May smiled, stepping through the crowd to the back of the café where a chair awaited her. 'It's lovely to see you all here.' As she sat May waved to Alice, the owner, who stood behind the counter serving customers. She smiled and waved back, nodding an invitation to begin.

'I'm really honoured you all came, and even bought my book.' May grinned, still amazed that people actually bought something she'd written and sold all by herself. 'So, well, while you're enjoying Alice's yummy cakes, I thought I'd read you the first chapter of my book. I do hope you like it.'

Twenty minutes later everyone in The Tea Cup was clapping and May was beaming. She signed books, smiled, spoke individually to everyone, gave them advice and help when they asked for it, and wondered how on earth her life had worked out this way.

She could hardly believe that it was less than two years ago that she'd been so unhappy she could barely get out of bed in the morning. When she'd sat in her own café, devouring croissants in a guilt-laden frenzy, desperately wondering why she couldn't win a battle of wills with a chocolate fudge cake and trying not to sob at the sight of her cake-rounded belly under her apron. When every day she'd tried to impose a strict diet on herself, and every day she'd succumbed to temptation. When she'd tried to write, to find fulfilment in words, but couldn't find the time, energy or creativity to do anything more than simply get through her day. When she'd been in love with the tall, blond and heart-stoppingly gorgeous Jake, the one she pursued even though she knew he could never love her, and the one she drove away with her neediness and desperation.

She couldn't believe that now, despite what Rose had warned, all that was behind her and now she was actually able to help those going through the same things she'd finally triumphed over. Such was May's delight, such was her gratification at touching the lives and hearts of all these women, that it eclipsed her worries about Ben and her dream with Rose. And when she'd finally finished chatting to readers and thanking Alice, May decided to hold onto the feeling of gratification and use the focus of helping others to push all her fears aside. Which, she was rather surprised to discover, wasn't too hard at all.

'Hi, honey, I'm home,' May called out as she stepped into the flat. An almighty crash came from the kitchen, and what sounded like the entire contents of the pots and pans cupboard clattered to the floor. Ben ran out of the kitchen, skidding along the wooden floors and colliding with May as she closed the door behind her.

'Wow, what's up?' May smiled at him as he danced from one foot to the other, looking into his big brown eyes lit up with excitement.

'I have amazing news,' Ben exclaimed, 'absolutely amazing news.'

'Oh?' May asked, wanting to kiss him. 'What – what is it?'

'Sit down.' Ben took May's hand and led her over to the sofa. 'You've got to be sitting down for this.'

May followed, wondering what he was so excited about, wishing the moment would last forever and almost believing that it could, no matter what Rose had said. May sat while Ben stood in front of her, clasping her hands and jumping from one foot to the other. She gazed up at him expectantly and suddenly Ben stood perfectly still.

'May,' he said softly, 'I think I've found you a publisher.'

May paced up and down the pavement outside The Tea Cup, where she'd arranged to meet the publisher for coffee and cake. Not that she'd be able to eat a single thing. Her stomach was rumbling now and May wished she could shut it up, but she was so nauseous with nerves she couldn't.

It had taken a moment or two for Ben's words to sink in. They'd hovered in the air like hummingbirds, fluttering bright and beautiful, far too fast to hold. But the beating of their wings echoed in May's ears and finally she'd been able to focus and listen to his story. The woman had walked into Ben's bookshop that afternoon, and they'd started to chat about books: their favourites, the ones they'd read at least ten times over, the few they'd never finished. At some point in the conversation Ben had boasted about May's debut work of self-published fiction and was delighted to discover the woman had already read and loved it.

'Well, it does have a permanent post in the window,' he'd said, smiling at May, 'and I do promote it at least once a week.'

'Yes, yes, you're wonderful and amazing and the very best boyfriend in the whole wide world.' May grinned. 'Now, what did she say next?'

Ben explained that the woman ran a small company: Insight & Inspiration Publishing, dedicated to books she believed would help transform the world, 'or at least the hearts and minds of those who read them.' And she thought May's could be one such book.

'She wants to meet you tomorrow,' Ben had said, 'if you're free.'

'If I'm free?' May had squealed, jumping up and down on the sofa, while Ben laughed. '*If* I'm free?'

They'd danced around the living room and when she'd finally stopped squealing May had given Ben deep, soft kisses that lasted long into the night.

May glanced at her watch and stood still. She was still twenty-three and a half minutes early, and if she kept marching up and down the pavement she'd pass out before the publisher even arrived. So, deciding to go inside, sit and try to calm down, May opened the door and went in.

'I'm here to meet a real live publisher,' May explained to Alice, who stood behind the counter, cutting a cake.

'As opposed to a fake, imaginary one?' Alice smiled, handed her a slice of hazelnut chocolate cake that May knew, given the still topsy-turvy nature of her stomach, would go horribly to waste.

'Well, there have been a fair few of those, believe me,' May said, remembering her old life and the endless hours daydreaming and fantasising about one day being published. Fantasies that, of course, also included marrying Jake and being able to indulge in vast quantities of chocolate cake without putting on a single pound.

'Take the table next to the window,' Alice suggested. 'Sit in the chair next to the wall. It's lucky. A lot of very fantastic things have happened to people sitting in that chair. It's had more than its share of marriage proposals, let me tell you.'

'Really?' May asked, wide-eyed, her heart quickening as she thought of Ben. They'd never talked about that, though she thought about it, hoped for it often enough. She was nervous about the subject that might follow it though: children. When her mother died May developed a fear of becoming a mother herself. She worried that she wouldn't be enough, that she wouldn't know what to do and how to do it right and, since she wouldn't be able to go to her own incredible mother for help, she might scar them for life. And that she couldn't quite bear.

'Yep.' Alice handed her a cappuccino. 'And now the chair can have its first ever book deal. How cool.'

'Oh, well, I don't know about that,' May mumbled, desperately trying not to get her hopes up too much in case they were soon to come crashing down in disappointment. 'I hope, I wish, but… we'll see.'

After May settled herself into the lucky chair, trying to swallow some cake and silence her rumbling belly, the next seventeen and a half minutes were the longest of her life. She tapped her finger on the table, crumbled the cake into a pile of crumbs and gazed out of the window, trying to distract herself from her nerves.

At ten past twelve exactly a short, slim woman, with shiny blonde hair in a pixie cut that highlighted her big green eyes, stepped into the café. Before she reached the counter she stopped and glanced around the room. Then, spotting May at the window, smiled and turned to walk to her.

'You, I see from the photo on your book jacket, must be May.' She reached out her hand. 'I'm Olivia Greene, but call me Lily.'

May stood, trying not to tremble, and she shook Lily's hand and smiled.

'It's lovely to meet you, Lily.' May forced herself to stop grinning, lest the publisher think she was a crazy person, and gently let go of her hand, though she wanted to hold on tight and kiss it.

Half an hour later they were sitting together, drinking coffee and chatting, while sunlight shone through the window, bathing them both in a warm glow.

'Lily was my mother's name,' May said, because she didn't know what else to say and because she'd been thinking about it since yesterday.

'I remember reading that in your book,' Lily said, smiling, 'but didn't know if it was true or not. I wondered how much of it was autobiographical.'

'Almost all of it,' May admitted. 'I suppose perhaps I don't have much of an imagination.'

'Oh, I doubt that,' Lily said, 'and anyway, it takes courage to write like that, to expose your heart for everyone else to see.'

'Well, to be honest,' May said, 'I never really imagined very many people ever would. When I sold my hundredth book I was so surprised I –'

'You know,' Lily interrupted, laughing, 'if you want to make it over here, you might want to acquire a bit of shameless self-confidence. We don't really do self-deprecating modesty and all that. After all, how can you expect other people to believe in you, if you don't even believe in yourself?'

'Yes, I see, of course.' May nodded, rather worried she might have just put Lily off entirely. 'I understand.'

'Good.' Lily settled back in her chair. 'I'm glad. Especially since your book is so much about teaching women courage and confidence, it'd be a little unfair if you didn't live like that yourself. And I wouldn't want to be the only one of us who believes in you.'

'Really?' May's eyes widened. 'You do? Yes, well, and I, um, I do too.'

May maintained an earnest gaze until Lily winked and they both burst into simultaneous giggles. May relaxed after that and they talked until long after The Tea Cup had officially closed, and Alice had retired to the kitchen to clean. They discovered they shared many similarities: personally, emotionally, historically… But underneath all the words lay an unspoken sense of connection, there since the moment they'd met and that only deepened the longer they sat together. Lily was delighted the young author was every bit as lovely as her prose. And May felt, for the first time in fourteen years, that she'd met someone who had the same spirit as her mother.

'We should go,' Lily said finally. 'I think we might have outstayed our welcome.'

'Yes,' May said, feeling as though she was on a date she didn't want to end. 'I suppose we should.'

After thanking their host, they stepped outside into darkness, onto a street lined with trees and fairy lights. They stood for a little while outside the café, chatting under the glow of a bright full moon that hung low in the sky. When they both started to shiver in the autumn breeze, they at last hugged goodbye. Lily crossed the road to her car and May turned to walk the thirty blocks home, waving at Alice through the window and giving her the thumbs up with both hands.

They'd decided to meet the next day at Lily's offices, where they'd sign the contract. The book would be published in six months. Lily would advance May a few thousand dollars and apply to extend her visa under the employment programme. She had it all covered. And in six short months *Men, Money and Chocolate* would be in bookshops all over America, or at least parts of it. Now thousands of women would have the chance to read May's story, to hopefully find inspiration and comfort in its twists and turns. May might lift their hearts and bring a little joy into their lives. Just the thought of it made her giddy.

As she meandered home, gazing up at the moon through the shifting clouds May felt as though she was looking at the floor of heaven: luminous cracked marble scattered with bright pinpricks of light. And she hoped her mother was gazing down at her, grinning from ear to ear to witness the happiest day of her daughter's life.

WISDOM

'We'll have the book launch here,' Ben said, 'won't we?'

'Of course we will,' May replied, laughing. 'Where else could it be? This is the only place in the world I'd have it, even if they offered me the Empire State Building.'

Ben smiled. 'I'm not sure they hold book launches there, but I'm touched you want it here. I'll invite every customer I've ever had and every single person I've ever met. You bake five hundred cupcakes and we'll be set.'

'I still can't believe it.' May beamed. 'I still can't quite believe it.'

It was two months until Publication Day, and May could hardly think about anything else. Conversations about book covers, manuscript edits, reading dates, tours and publicity left little room for other topics.

Ben was wonderful throughout it all. He listened to every concern she had, read through all the edits she wanted to make, helped to plan events, even called magazine and newspaper editors when May was too shy. For her part May continued to work in the bookshop, although she often came late and left early to do something or other connected with her book. She'd kiss Ben on the cheek as she was flying in or out and thank him yet again for everything. She still held her twice-weekly cake and inspiration evenings, but everything else they'd done together was put on hold. And he noticed, as the weeks and months went by, that she flew out faster and no longer stopped to let her lips linger for long. He began to feel himself pushed to the edge of May's world, and the only sure-fire way he could get her attention any more was to talk about the book. But Ben understood that the realisation of a life-long dream always needed to be honoured, and he believed the obsession would settle down into pure passion once May saw her books on shelves and knew that the dream wasn't an illusion after all. When she had really done it. When it had come true. Then Ben imagined May would start writing again; they would go out on dates again, make love more often and even have entire conversations that had absolutely nothing to do with literature or helping the female population with their love lives or weight worries at all. And until that day he would wait. Although he had to admit that, after almost four months of this, that day couldn't come soon enough.

'Hum, it's still not quite right,' May mused. 'What if we make the gold lettering shiny instead of matt?'

It was long past midnight. Lily and May had been staring at the new book cover proofs for the last five hours, batting ideas back and forth.

'I really liked the other one by that other author,' May said, waving one hand towards the computer.

'With the moon – can't we make it more like that?'

'Sure,' Lily said sleepily, 'sure we can. But…'

'But?' May looked up.

'Why don't we talk about it tomorrow?'

'Yeah, okay, of course. I'll study more covers, other authors' websites, and bring you more ideas. It needs to be noticeable, so women pick it off the shelves, so they read it.' May thought of her Tuesday and Thursday night audiences. 'Otherwise it'll be wasted, which would be such a shame. I really think it might touch a lot of lives, help a lot of people. I don't mean to be arrogant, 'cause it's not really about me; it's about them. I never thought it possible before, but now I see how it touches the women who love it and… anyway, what time shall I come over?'

'Honey.' Lily reached across the table and placed her palm over May's, giving it a gentle squeeze. 'I echo your feelings for wanting to help the whole world entirely – that's why I'm publishing your wonderful little book – but you're in danger of having your altruistic impulses corrupted by obsessing and thinking about it all too much. Also, given the lures of any venture into fame and fortune, no matter how slight, you must be careful about not getting sucked into the wild and not-at-all-wonderful world of Comparison, Control and Crazy. I think you might want to let go a little. Stop thinking about it. Step back. Why don't you take a few days off?'

'What?' May frowned, nervous. 'Why? I'm fine. Aren't we fine? I thought we were fine.'

Lily just looked at her with a kind smile. May bit her lip, puzzling.

'What do you mean anyway?' May asked. 'About the not-at-all-wonderful world of Comparison, Con–'

'Comparison, Control and Crazy,' Lily finished, 'is the world you step into whenever you leave your private comfort zone for the public arena. You stop to survey your surroundings; you take a look around to see who's out there in the public eye with you. And if you're not careful you lose yourself completely in comparing yourself to those materially more successful than you. Then in an attempt to gain back your sanity you lose yourself even more by desperately trying to control everything, especially those things you have absolutely no hope of controlling: like how popular you are, how many books you sell, or how many friends you have on Facebook. Just everyday ridiculous things like that. And after a few weeks is when the crazy settles in… And, sadly, by then you might have been so corrupted that you've forgotten all about wanting to help people, the reason you started in the first place.'

'I won't forget,' May said. 'I don't even want to be famous. I can't imagine anything more embarrassing.'

'Yes, my love, I know that's true,' Lily said. 'I know that's who you really are and it's one of the many reasons I love you. But fame is a drug that few are immune to. It's like a daily dose of heroin and it's nearly impossible not to get addicted.'

'Well, but –' May looked a little panicked. 'But surely I can control those things. I can publicise my book, invite people to events, do readings, TV, magazines, and just focus on *why* I'm doing it and not get lost in…'

'Oh, my dear, sweet May,' Lily said, 'I hope so, but I worry for you anyway, and I have to tell you now while you're still innocent and uncorrupted. Because if you do become addicted to the fame drug, then you'll stop listening to anything Ben or I might say. You'll become a completely different person, not lovely little May any more.'

'No,' May said. 'No, I can't. I won't let that happen. Never. Not in a million years.'

'I'm sure you wouldn't want it to, but such drugs can corrupt the purest of us. We can all lose our souls and our centres in the desire for things like love, popularity, wealth, chocolate…' Lily winked. 'Didn't you write a book about that?'

May managed a smile. 'Yes, of course, I know what you mean. I just think, well, I've learnt my lessons there and I wouldn't make those mistakes again.'

'I know you'll try,' Lily said, 'and I know you wrote the book both to do something courageous and then to help other women in their own lives. You were doing it for self-fulfilment rather than success, which is right and wonderful. But as you carry on down the path, making choices about what to do now and next, remember always to ask yourself if it's an impulse that springs from the purity of your heart, or from the desires and demands of your mind.'

May sat back in her chair. 'What do you mean?'

'The mind tells you what you want,' Lily said, 'and often those things are pieced together from what you think is wrong with you and your life. So you want to fix it. If you want fame and fortune because you don't think your life is enough as it is, and you don't think that you're perfect just as you are, then it will only end in heartache. If you don't get enough of it – and it'll never be enough then – you're unhappy, and if you get it you're unhappy too. Because, as you well know, self-fulfilment might precede success, but it's never a product of it.'

'Why?' May asked. 'Why does it work like that?'

'Because those desires go against the wisdom of the heart.'

'What's that?'

'The heart has true desires that have nothing to do with making you a better person, or your life a better life,' Lily explained. 'The heart only expresses itself; it doesn't want anything more than that. Just to be heard. Just to reach out and touch others; that's all it wants.'

'Yes,' May said, 'that was why I wrote my book. I mean, it wasn't even as if *I* wrote it but my heart. It sort of came through me…'

'Well, exactly. You know, when I was a lil' girl growing up in Austin, Texas,' Lily said with an affected drawl, 'the Girl Scouts had a motto they drummed into us. I learnt it by heart the first moment they told us, 'cause it was just about the most beautiful thing I'd ever heard. *What you have,* they said, *is your gift from God. And what you do with what you have is your gift to God.*'

'Wow,' May said. 'That's beautiful.'

'Isn't it? To me it means that we're meant to ask what life wants from us, just as often as asking life for what we want from it. That's the wisdom of the heart rather than the demands of the mind, and I try to live my life that way, whenever I possibly can.' Lily smiled. 'So what do you say we wrap this little party up and go home and get some sleep?'

'Yes.' May sighed softly. 'I think that sounds like a very good idea.'

That night May curled up next to Ben, squeezing him tightly.

'I'm sorry I haven't been paying you much attention,' she whispered, kissing his cheek. Ben shifted in his sleep. 'I'll come back to you now. I won't get lost in the crazy world out there. I'll always stay true to my heart, and yours, I promise.'

'What if nobody comes?' May paced up and down the bookshop floor, wiping her sweaty hands on her soft pink silk dress. 'What if absolutely nobody turns up and we have to eat five hundred cupcakes all by ourselves?'

'Well,' Ben said, 'would that be such a very bad thing?'

May smiled. 'You jest, but that used to be about my weekly consumption when I was running the café,' she said. 'And now I'd rip my very beautiful but very tight little dress open, and that —'

'Would be a *very* wonderful thing.' Ben grinned, picking May up and twirling her round and round. She giggled while he carried her to the enormous display of cupcakes: hundreds of red, purple and gold cakes sparkling with glitter and shiny frosting. May had spent two days in the kitchen carefully creating each one, piping on the icing, sprinkling the glitter, cutting little hearts and gold coins and chocolate bars out of marzipan, decorating the cupcakes with symbols of men, money and chocolate. They were little pieces of perfection and

Ben hoped, more desperately than he'd ever hoped for anything in his life, that two hundred people would show up to eat them.

They both looked up, necks practically snapping out of their sockets, as the bell above the door tinkled and in walked Alice and her boyfriend. Ben whispered a small prayer of thanks and hoped the next time the door opened it would be twenty people walking through, not just two.

In the end the night was a glorious success. Beyond even Ben's wildest dreams. Well over two hundred people had shown up. All the cupcakes had been eaten, all the champagne finished, all the books signed and sold. At the end of the evening, when every guest had staggered out, full of cake, wine and words, Lily had declared it the best, by far the most beautiful and brilliant, book launch of any book she'd ever published.

As Ben finally locked the door, and May slid to the floor with a beatific smile fixed to her face, they looked at each other.

'I only wish Faith could have come,' May said. 'I miss her. I'd have loved her to be here. But other than that it was a most perfect night.'

'I hope I can meet her one day, this wonderfully kooky cousin of yours,' Ben said. 'I guess we'll have to wait a little while until we've got a bit more cash. When your book's a bestseller you can fly us over to jolly old England first class and I can meet your whole family.'

'I wouldn't hold your breath.' May laughed. 'I think there's about as much chance of that as Faith becoming the first millionaire astrologer-psychic-modern dancer in England.'

Ben smiled 'Well, we'll see about that. But this wasn't a bad show, was it?'

'Not bad at all.' May sighed happily. 'Those books, all those women. I might just be able to make a difference in the world after all.'

'Yes,' Ben said, 'that's lovely, but don't forget about you and me while you're out there saving the world.'

'Of course not.' May started scattering Ben with little kisses. 'I could never forget about you – you're the loveliest, most special, beautiful, wonderful, most precious person in my life.'

In that moment Ben felt such a surge of joy and love in his heart that he couldn't contain it. At least that was the only way he could explain what happened next.

'Do you want kids?' he asked suddenly, softly, with such desire in his words it was clear that he wanted them right now this minute, if at all possible.

'What?' May stared at him, shocked.

Ben hesitated. He stepped back. He'd been wrong. He'd misread her signals. It was too soon for this subject. He'd scared her off. He quickly wracked his brains for a seamless shift into another topic of conversation.

'I, um, I... I don't know,' he mumbled. 'I meant to say, I... would you like to dance?'

May smiled and nodded, relieved, not knowing what she would have said otherwise. Ben stood, reached for May's hand and pulled her to her feet. He held her close to his chest and stroked the silk of her dress. Slowly he started to move and hum the words of their song. She smiled up at him, happy to be in his arms, exhausted and glad he was holding her up. Ben touched his lips to the top of her head and told himself that if he just kept holding her then everything was going to be all right.

FORGIVENESS

'I'm going to be on TV, I'm going to be on TV!' May shouted, running through the bookshop, reaching Ben, unpacking boxes of books in the back. 'Can you believe it? I can't believe it, I can't believe it!'

'That's fantastic, love, really fantastic,' Ben said, still unpacking.

May stopped and looked at him. 'Didn't you hear what I said?'

'I think,' he replied, meeting her eyes, 'everyone in a five-block radius did.'

'What do you mean?' May frowned. 'Shouldn't I be excited? Isn't it amazing news? I don't understand why you aren't happy for me.'

'It is amazing and I am happy for you,' Ben said, though he didn't *really* sound it. 'So when's the show?'

'In two weeks. Lily called some producers ages ago and they've suddenly got an opening in three weeks' time. The programme is about women who've followed their dreams at all costs and made them come true. Loads of people will be watching. It's a great opportunity to get the word out, to tell so many women about the book, to help give them the courage and inspiration to follow their own dreams. Just think about it; I can really do some good. It's totally wonderful!'

'Yes,' Ben agreed. 'It really is.'

May frowned at him again. 'What's wrong?'

But this time it was Ben who wasn't brave enough to be honest. How could he say he was jealous? It sounded so unreasonable. He *was* proud of May, that she was realising her dreams, pursuing her passions. He was touched that she cared so deeply about helping other women who were going through what she'd suffered. But all that didn't stop him wishing May would give him a little more time and attention. Since the book launch, she'd been in such demand that they'd hardly been out together in weeks. Women came looking for her at the shop, spending hours telling her their problems and seeking advice. To reach more people May had increased her evening gatherings to four nights a week. She received endless amounts of emails that she stayed up long into the night answering. They hadn't made love in quite a while. But, feeling it was not fair of him to complain, sadly Ben decided to say nothing.

'I'm fine.' Ben smiled. 'Really, I am. I'm very happy. It's great.'

May kissed him. 'Okay, that's good. I'm glad.' Of course she could tell he wasn't, not really. For a start, the smile hadn't reached his eyes. But she didn't know what to do about it and, truthfully, didn't want him to bring her down. So sadly May didn't say anything either.

Two days later, as preparations for the TV show were fully underway, with May practising what she'd say in front of the mirror for hours on end, Ben had persuaded her to sit down for a quick dinner. And all through it he tried to suppress the knots of fear and frustration twisting inside his belly. But it was no good. He couldn't eat and he could barely look May in the eye.

'What's going on?' May finally sighed, unable to ignore it any longer. 'What's wrong? What have I done? And don't tell me "nothing".'

'It's not just about you,' Ben said, trying to remain calm but feeling a few months' worth of frustration boiling up inside him and bubbling over. 'Wait, I'm sorry, that's not true. It *is* all about you, all the time.'

'What's that supposed to mean?' May frowned.

'Oh, I think it's pretty clear. I've spent the last six months listening to you talk endlessly about the book, thinking about nothing else,' Ben snapped. 'All you seem to care about is all the women you can help, these strangers who need you. Which is very virtuous of you and everything, but –'

'I'm trying to do something good,' May cut in. 'I want to give something back for all I've been given. How can that be a bad thing?'

'It's not,' Ben said, 'and I know I sound like an asshole, but I don't care any more. I know those women need you, but I need you too. And I feel like I'm losing you.'

May stared at him, utterly shocked. 'What? You're not losing me. This is just something I've got to do. It won't be forever. It's just –'

'Won't it?' Ben asked. 'And when's it going to stop? When you've saved the whole world?'

'No, of course not,' May replied, though she couldn't say that she would ever stop; when, after all, would her efforts be enough? She stood and started pacing up and down the kitchen. 'Look, I thought this was what people in love, partners, did. They supported each other; they cared about someone other than themselves. Isn't that the whole point of love?'

'Yes,' Ben said, 'and I did, I *do*. For the first few months, at least, and then for the last few it's been harder, and now I'm starting to wonder if it's ever going to be about "us" again, or if it's always going to be about them, about you.'

'Oh, come on,' May said. Though she could hear herself being defensive and unsympathetic, she felt threatened and couldn't stop herself. 'For centuries women have been doing nothing but supporting men, standing behind them, listening endlessly and helping in every way, completely subjugating themselves… and when a man is asked to do the same, he can't, *can he?*'

'Hey,' Ben said softly. 'It's not like that, not at all. I don't want you to do that. And I know it wasn't fair. I know history wasn't fair to women, but that's not what it's like with us; that's not the point. It's not about being equals; it's about being connected, about knowing each other intimately, but you haven't asked about me, how I'm feeling, for so long. And I can't remember the last time we made love.'

'Don't be silly,' May said. 'It was only, only last…'

'Yes?' Ben said, triumphant. 'When?'

'Oh, for goodness sake, is sex all that matters?' May stopped pacing, put her palms on the table and stared at Ben, her face flushed with fury. Deep, deep down she knew she was being unreasonable and Ben had a point, but that only made her more angry. 'I threw my love and my life away on a man once,' May cried. 'I gave up on everything I ever wanted. I made him the whole and entire reason I got up in the morning. And it all went to shit –'

'Oh, yes.' Ben sighed. 'The famous amazing Jake, the guy who fucked you up and left me to pick up the pieces –'

'Shut up, shut up!' May shouted, remembering how desperate she'd felt, how hollow and bereft, as though her core, her very sense of self, had unravelled, twisting and contorting itself in a crazy, vain bid to keep hold of Jake. And how, when he'd finally left her, she'd completely fallen apart, feeling completely empty and alone, having lost her love and herself. 'That was the worst mistake I ever made and I'm not doing it again. Okay? I'm never doing it again!'

May glared at Ben and he just looked back at her, shocked into silence. Not knowing what else to say or do, May turned and ran out of the room. A moment later Ben heard the front door slam.

As she stood on the street, her heart racing and tears running down her cheeks, May felt a surge of regret in her heart. She wanted to run back up to Ben and bury herself in his arms. But she was scared too. She really couldn't bear to make the same mistake with him as she'd made with Jake. She didn't think her heart would survive being smashed all over again – even though May knew that Ben wasn't the same as Jake, even though she knew he really loved her, all of her, even when she was being needy and neurotic, no matter what. Rationally she knew that, but, underneath it all, she was still scared.

So May stood on the street and, not knowing what to do next, just started walking. After about an hour she stopped and looked around. It was a neighbourhood she didn't know, quite scruffy but almost quaint, with unique boutiques scattered up and down the street. Most of them needed repainting and brightening up a bit, but all in all it felt like a safe place to catch one's breath, a safe place to stop and think, and a safe place to just be. May walked a few steps and leant against the doorframe of an old sweet shop, no longer trading but still with all its wares in the window: glass jars of SweeTarts, Lemon Drops, Jaw Breakers and Candy Hearts. May stared into the window for a while. Soft memories of childhood delight bubbled up inside her and, for a few forgetful moments, she was seven years old again, gripping her mother's hand and gazing up over the counter at the array of rainbow colours that greeted her: treats of all shapes and sizes, one of which she would be allowed to choose and consume, with sticky fingers and sugar-coated lips, on their way home.

May looked up from the window to the faded sign that said 'Just Sweet Enough' in long loping letters and creaked in a gust of wind. As she gazed at it May considered whether or not she should carry on walking, but for some reason she wanted to stay. So she sat down on the pavement, among the mess of squashed cardboard boxes and assorted sticky sweet wrappers, still too upset with Ben to care about the dirt.

Just then a rustling a few feet away made May sit up. A man had emerged from underneath a pile of cardboard boxes. May stared at him, eyes wide. He didn't look at her, but proceeded to pick specks of lint off his trousers. May glanced away, fixing her gaze straight ahead, her whole body stiff. She wanted to leave, as fast as possible, but she didn't want to offend the man and possibly incur his wrath. So she stayed still, waiting for a good moment to make her getaway.

Eventually, when all the lint was dispensed with, the man turned to her. 'Who are *you*?' he asked.

'I'm, sorry. I didn't mean to disturb you. I was just, just –' May searched for the closest word to the truth – 'resting. I'll go.'

May got ready to stand, but the old man waved her down.

'Please, stay.' The homeless man reached out his hand. 'I'm Harry.'

She took it and replied, 'May.'

'So, May, what's a nice young lady like you doing in a place like this?'

'Oh.' She glanced around. 'I don't know, it doesn't seem like such a bad place to be.'

'Well, yes, it's one of the better places in the city. More often than not it's home to me, but it doesn't seem like home to you.'

'I, well, you see –' but May was too tired to lie so she plumped for the truth – 'I just had a big fight with my boyfriend. I ran out of the house. I didn't know what else to do, so I suppose I just kept going…'

'Well, that's a natural enough reaction to conflict: the flight-or-fight response,' Harry said, 'though sadly not at all a helpful one.'

'Yes,' May admitted, 'I can see that now. I just, I was so upset I couldn't stand it. I just wanted it all to go away, so I guess… I guess I went away instead.'

'You know, in fifty-one years of marriage,' Harry said, stretching out his legs, 'my wife and I, well, we fought often enough, but we made a point never to let our outbursts last more than half an hour. To the minute. And they never did. We always made up quickly, let it – whatever it was – go and went back to listening to and loving each other. That way we never had the chance to inflict irreparable damage. And, the thing is, we never really needed more than half an hour, even if we really wanted to keep fighting at the time. And the next day we'd barely remember what it was that upset us in the first place. Funny that, isn't it?'

'Really?' May stared at him, incredulous. 'That's amazing.'

'Yes, she was, when we were together. Edith was my whole life.' Harry smiled wistfully. 'My very reason for happiness. We worked together every day and never spent a night apart.'

'Wow,' May said. 'That's… wow.'

'This was our shop.' Harry nodded up at Just Sweet Enough and let out a little sigh. 'I had to re-mortgage it when she got sick. Health insurance wouldn't cover it. Then… it was repossessed last year, three months after Edith died.'

'O-oh,' May stammered, tears in her eyes. 'I'm sorry. I'm so sorry.'

Harry laughed. 'I had more love in my lifetime than most have in twenty. I was always the luckiest man I knew. Now the winter of my life has stripped me bare with loss. But, all in all, given the life I've had, I'm still one of the luckiest men alive.'

'That's beautiful,' May said, feeling her shoulders relaxing and some of the tension seeping out of her. 'But it's not just luck, is it? To have a love like that, I mean. You must have worked really hard to have it.'

'Oh, we didn't work so very hard,' Harry said. 'We just watched out for a few things. We made each other a few promises and stuck to them. That's all.'

'Like what?' May blurted out, before realising he might think her a little rude. 'If you don't mind me asking.'

'Oh, of course not.' Harry smiled. 'I'm always happy to help out a lovely young lady in distress.'

May blushed a little in the darkness.

'First, we always told each other the truth, no matter how scary it seemed to be. And it was always our own truth, from our point of view. We took responsibility for the way we felt inside; we didn't blame each other for it.'

May squinted at him, trying to understand.

'That's where most couples go wrong, you see. They blame their partners for the way they feel,' Harry explained. 'Of course it's easy enough to do. Especially since our partners know exactly what to say to trigger our sadness, pain or anger. And when they do, and we react, we blame them. So they defend themselves, and then we're fighting them.'

'But it sort of is their fault, isn't it?' May asked. 'I mean, if they try to trigger our anger or pain on purpose…'

'Oh, but you see "fault" is already a fighting concept; it's already putting you on opposing teams instead of the same one. I'm suggesting that if we take responsibility for the way we feel, then we won't react to people in the same way; we'll be able to see them without hate or blame and then we'll be able to understand *why* they are trying to hurt us. Then we'll be able to help heal them, us, the relationship, the whole kit-'n'-caboodle.'

'Well.' May smiled. 'I suppose that's a nice way of looking at it. I –'

'It's the *only* way of looking at it,' Harry said, 'if you want to actually live a life instead of fight a war. If you want to feel loved and blessed, then it's the thing to do. Of course, not everyone does. Some people like the fight, but I just leave them to it.'

'I know I was wrong today,' May admitted, 'I think I've been wrong for a while. It's just… I got a little lost in my own thing and forgot about him. And I wanted to be independent, not to lose myself in a relationship like I did before, but this time I guess I went too far the other way.'

'Well, that's where forgiveness comes in,' Harry said, 'and empathy. And compassion. All essential ingredients in any marriage.'

May nodded. 'Yes, I suppose so. Not that we're married though.'

'Oh, living in sin, eh?' Harry raised an eyebrow in mock shock. 'Well, the way Edith and I lived, we always gave each other the benefit of the doubt. We didn't take the other person's behaviour personally, and we let things go, almost even before they'd happened. So if I was in a bad mood about something, she'd simply wait until it passed. And if she was feeling bad, if she was rude to me, the first thing I always did was ask her what was wrong.'

'That's amazing,' May said. 'No wonder you were so happy.'

'We just decided to put the relationship first,' Harry explained, 'which meant that we both won. But when you're fighting one of you is going to lose. Which, of course, ultimately means you both lose.'

May nodded again, thinking about how she'd left Ben at home, how she'd tried to hurt him simply because she was feeling hurt.

'When it comes to forgiveness, remember this,' Harry said. 'In a marriage, in any relationship, both partners have their point of view; both believe themselves to be right. Otherwise there would be no fight. So you can always use empathy and compassion to stop an argument before it begins. When your partner is behaving badly you can try to ask why, instead of immediately defending yourself.

If a usually kind person is shouting, or being rude, it's invariably because they're in some sort of pain and they just don't know how to express themselves in any other way.'

May sighed. 'I wish I'd done that tonight.' She began to realise just how much she'd been losing herself and neglecting her relationship in her single-minded focus on her own personal cause.

'Don't forget to forgive yourself,' Harry said, smiling, 'or you'll just end up punishing your boyfriend again. After all, there's nothing quite so unattractive and depressing as a little self-loathing, is there?'

May returned his smile. 'No, I suppose not.'

As she looked at him, Harry started to pull himself up until he was standing, leaning against the wall for support. 'And now, my dear,' he said, 'I'm afraid I must go.'

'Oh?' May said. 'Why? Where?'

'I have a long-standing dinner order with the very generous owner of a lovely little patisserie on Height Street,' Harry said, 'and the window of opportunity is a small one.'

'Gosh, well, yes, of course,' May said. 'And I suppose I really should go home. I have some apologising to do, some forgiveness to ask for.'

'Wonderful.' Harry reached out his hand. 'And I wish you well.'

'Thank you,' May said, trying to postpone the moment, not wanting to see him go. 'Thank you for everything.' And then, suddenly quite overwhelmed with gratitude and not having any other way to say it, May jumped up, took his hand and gave him a kiss on the cheek for saving her life. Or, at the very least, her heart. Then she pulled him into a hug. And while she held him May slipped all the money she had into his jacket pocket.

If she'd been fit enough, May would have run the thirty blocks home. As it was she hurried, scurried and crawled. She pushed open the front door, panting, ran the final few steps through the bookshop, up the spiral staircase and into the kitchen where she found Ben still sitting at the table, staring off into space.

'I'm so, so, so sorry, sweetheart,' May said, as he looked up. 'I didn't mean, well, I did, because I really lost my way and…'

Ben smiled and opened his arms and May, wondering for a moment if he had psychically attended Harry's forgiveness seminar, ran round the table and rushed right into him, almost knocking them both over.

'I love you, I love you, I love you,' May gushed, kissing him all over his cheeks, his neck, his hair…

'I love you too, you crazy girl,' Ben said, laughing. 'Welcome back.'

FAME

May was back and, for the next few weeks, everything was fine. Life resumed as normal and May made concerted efforts to really be with Ben when she was with him, instead of getting distracted by thoughts of her book and the upcoming TV show. Of course, with life always being a learning experience, she didn't succeed all the time. But whenever Ben saw May getting distracted, lost in fantasies of the future, he gently brought her back by saying something funny or giving her magnificent kisses that left her blinking and wondering what day of the week it was.

It seemed as though nothing would rock their relationship. But then, as is so often the case, the next challenge came along. If only, May would later think, the TV show had happened later. If only they'd had longer to cement the newfound trust, forgiveness, compassion and empathy between them. If only she'd known better than to make the same mistake twice. But, of course life doesn't work with 'if only', and perhaps that's just as well or there'd be reason to be lost in regret all the time.

As the day of the TV show dawned, May and Ben pottered around, practising real love in the face of imperfection, with no idea how hard they were about to be hit. The morning was a beautiful one. Sunlight streamed in through the windows and May, unable to sleep from nerves, had got up early to make fresh coffee and bake blueberry scones, even though it wasn't Sunday. They ate breakfast together, May excited and terrified about her upcoming appearance on national television and Ben proud and reassuring her she'd be wonderful.

Three hours and twelve dress changes later, they were driving across town in Ben's cream-and-black VW Bug.

'Hey, *bichana*, what time is Lily getting there?' he asked.

'An hour before the show,' May replied while chewing her fingernail. 'It's going to be awful, I'm going to freeze, I can't remember why I'm doing this.'

'Because you've written a beautiful book, inspirational and passionate, that is changing people's lives,' Ben reassured her, 'and you want to tell as many people about it as possible.'

'Oh yeah, that,' May said, letting herself smile a little. 'Now I remember: *what you have is your gift from God. And what you do with what you have is your gift to God.*'

'Exactly,' Ben said, 'and will you say that to the world when you get the chance? Tell me what you've been rehearsing for the last month.'

'Okay, right, yes.' May laughed. 'That I believe in miracles and magic and more than we can see... that life takes care of us if we let it. I don't understand tragedies, but I think a great deal of personal suffering is self-created. I believe in courage, compassion and connection – with long spoons – and that bringing joy to someone else is the biggest joy you'll ever have. And that's what I've always wanted to do with my book.'

'*Long spoons?*' Ben asked. 'That's new. Did you add it?'

'Oh, yes, that.' May smiled and said, 'Well, I heard this story once from some inspirational fellow. It was about heaven and how it's like a magnificent dinner party, every guest having one long spoon which they can't feed themselves with, only the person sitting across them at the table. So everyone has to feed everyone else. I remember thinking it was a wonderful metaphor about connection, taking care of people and what brings us the most joy.'

Ben watched the road, smiling to himself and wondering if he could possibly ever love the woman sitting next to him more than he did in that moment.

Six hours later they were back in the centre of San Francisco, walking along the pavement, hand in hand, on their way to a romantic dinner.

'I was okay, wasn't I?'

'You were magnificent, absolutely magnificent.'

'Really?' May asked. 'Really?'

Ben pulled her close and kissed her. 'Yes, for the millionth time, really.'

'I think I remembered to say everything I meant to,' May said. 'I talked a lot about courage, didn't I? Maybe a little too much, and about always having compassion for yourself, how finding your passion in life is the best diet there is… what else? Oh yes…'

While May chattered away, Ben touched the little ring box in the right-hand pocket of his trousers. He'd been carrying it around for three days and nights now, and wondered if tonight would be the night. He thought perhaps he should wait until tomorrow, since this meal was supposed to celebrate May's first ever TV appearance. But then perhaps a proposal would be the perfect end to a perfect day. At least that's what he hoped.

'What are you thinking about?'

'Oh, what? Sorry.' May's question brought Ben back. 'Nothing. I'm fine.'

'I'm not fine,' May said, grinning. 'I'm so completely and utterly happy, I can't quite believe it.' She turned to him. 'You know, I've decided I don't want to be a multi-million-dollar bestselling author.'

'Oh?' Ben raised a quizzical eyebrow.

'No,' May continued, 'I mean, I'd love for a million people to read *Men, Money and Chocolate* and have it support and inspire them all. But I don't want to be rich and famous. I don't want to be sucked into the world of Comparison, Control and Crazy –'

'Eh?' Ben frowned, wondering what on earth she was talking about and how much he'd missed while thinking about his proposal.

'Oh, it's just something Lily said…' May trailed off. 'Anyway, I love the life I have – with you, running the bookshop, hopefully helping the women who come to me, knowing what's real and what matters. I don't think I could handle fame and fortune anyway. Apparently it's like heroin: you get a stab of it and you're sucked into the unreality of a world where all that matters is success, appearances, being better and more brilliant than everyone else in the room.' May thought back to the days when she sat on her sofa eating boxes of cookies and tubs of ice cream. 'And, given how I used to be with chocolate, I don't think I'd stand much of a chance with heroin. Or cocaine…'

Ben gripped the little ring box, preparing himself, thinking this might be the perfect time. He'd just wait for her to finish.

'Maybe some people can handle it without losing their hearts and their heads, but I doubt I could.

I mean, we witnessed that last month, right, what I'm like when I lose myself in something.' May smiled. 'In fact you'd better watch out with me; I think I have a bit of an addictive personality. You should have seen me back in England when I was miserable and eating every cookie, croissant and chocolate cake in sight…'

Ben cleared his throat and opened his mouth to speak. But before he could say anything, May glanced up to see that they'd reached the restaurant.

'Hey, wonderful,' she said, grinning. 'We're here, I'm so hungry I could easily eat a whole chocolate cake right now.'

They fell through the doorway, laughing and stuffed full of food.

'I never said I had fat toes,' May objected, giggling. 'You're making it up.'

'Oh, yes, you did. I remember you wiggling your toes as you said it.'

'Well, since the show was live, it's my word against yours,' May said triumphantly, 'and I choose to believe mine.'

'Oh, didn't I tell you? I recorded it.' Ben rushed into the living room to the television. 'So now we'll know the truth.'

May ran after him and they both collapsed onto the sofa. She clutched her stomach, giggling. 'I ate far, far too much food. If I laugh again I think I'm gonna be sick.'

'Not on my red leather couch you're not,' Ben said. 'Hey, May, there's something I wanna ask you.'

'Okay.' May sat up a little, not for a moment suspecting what it was going to be. 'I'm listening.' Then her eye caught the flashing red light on the answer phone. 'Oh my goodness, we've got sixty-three messages!'

'What?' Ben sat up and peered at it. 'Who on earth…?'

'Maybe it's just from friends who saw me on TV today,' May sighed a little. 'Oh my goodness, how completely and utterly mortifying.' Though secretly she was really rather touched. 'Hey, maybe Faith called, which reminds me I must call her. But, sorry, what was it you wanted to say?'

'It can wait a sec. Let's listen to these first.' Ben pressed the playback button. And for the next ten minutes they heard messages from the assistants of every book agent, newspaper editor and TV producer in San Francisco and beyond. They'd all seen, or at least heard about, the show and they wanted to talk. They *loved* the book title. They *loved* May's story. And, of course, they *loved* May. After every single message had played, Ben and May turned to each other.

'Wow,' he said.

'Wow,' she said.

'It's pretty amazing,' Ben admitted. 'What are you going to do?'

May shrugged as though she hadn't really thought about it, as though she wasn't really considering it, as though it didn't matter much to her at all. 'I don't know.'

Ben felt a small puff of panic float up inside him. Trying hard not to show it on his face, he prayed he wasn't about to lose her all over again. 'Well…'

'Well, I suppose I should call them all back,' May reasoned. 'I mean, that's only polite, right?'

'Right.'

'And maybe, I mean, it'd probably be sensible to have an agent at least. Don't you think?'

'Sure.'

'And it might be worth getting a little more publicity for the book,' May mused. 'I mean, to get the message out there to as many women as possible.'

'Of course.'

Ben fingered the box in his pocket. He could see that she was pretty overwhelmed with all the attention. That she was basking in it. That it was just starting to sink in. May was happy. Indeed, though she was trying to play it down as much as possible, she was clearly overjoyed. And Ben could see that his own little declaration of love wasn't going to add very much to it. Now was not the right time. He would have to hold onto it for a little while longer.

The next month flew by in a flurry of phone calls, meetings, interviews, appearances, book signings and readings. Ben and May saw less and less of each other, and the gap between them grew wider. May, though she denied it to herself, became increasingly distracted by the demands of her newfound fame. And Ben started to feel that their relationship had devolved into something more akin to a chance meeting at a Hollywood party, with him trying anything to get her attention while May sneaked glances over his shoulder to see if anyone more important had just walked into the room.

At first May was oblivious to this, and Ben didn't bring it up. He hoped it would pass, that May would stay true to her word. He hoped the allure of fame and fortune would prove weaker than her love of their life together. But, unfortunately for them both, Ben underestimated the power of the drug that had beguiled May. Her addiction had returned, but this time the seductive nature of attention and adoration was far, far stronger than chocolate.

It didn't happen straight away. For a little while May kept her focus on her heart, her attention on spreading her message of courage and compassion and helping women with their struggles in life. The first few interviews were fine. The first few fans didn't turn May's head. The first few weeks of increasing interest, compliments and soaring book sales didn't knock May off centre too much. She still sat in the kitchen with Doughnut, reading the local paper, a little embarrassed whenever she saw her picture. She still took Ben coffee in the mornings and kissed him. She still sat at her desk, writing back to requests for advice and gazing out at the beautiful view of San Francisco.

But it didn't last. The stability of her relationship simply couldn't stand against the riptide that was slowly sucking May under. Her inner knowing, her intuition, her sense of self – they were still too soft for May to feel the little nudges that warned her against the mercurial nature, and false high, of fame and fortune. And by the time May realised the illusion of what she'd given a piece of her soul for, it was too late. She wanted it too much. The drug was in her system and she needed her next hit.

Now whenever Ben gently tried to bring up how lost and distracted she'd become, May fobbed him off with false words of wisdom, reassuring him that she knew exactly what she was doing, that she was entirely able to stop at any moment she chose. But Ben could see the look of desire in her eye when another magazine editor called, when her agent negotiated bigger and bigger deals for TV and public appearances, when she saw another pair of four-hundred-dollar shoes in a shop window, even though she already had six similar pairs.

It was Lily, who wasn't so scared of losing May's love, who finally confronted her. 'They want you wearing what?' she asked when May called to tell her about a photo shoot for a magazine.

'A corset,' May said. 'It's not like I'm going to be naked.'

'And you don't think it's a bit… provocative, demeaning and entirely unnecessary. You're a writer, not some sort of slutty film star.'

'Lil!' May gasped, having never heard her publisher be so rude.

'I'm sorry,' Lily said, 'but film stars are expected to take their clothes off, aren't they? And I'm pretty sure that writers are expected to keep them on. What does Ben think of this?'

'He's fine with it.'

'You haven't told him yet, have you?'

'No, but he will be,' May said. 'He's supportive.'

'He's scared of losing you,' Lily retorted, 'so he's making the mistake of not taking care of you, of not telling you what he really thinks. I hope that corset's supportive. Or you might be doing a topless spread.'

May laughed. 'Don't be silly, I'd never do that.'

'Oh?' Lily sounded sceptical. 'It seems to me that you're so lost in the fantasy world of fame and fortune right now that you'd trade in your morals, principles and integrity tomorrow if they offered you the cover of *Vogue*.'

May was silent, crushed by Lily's low opinion of her, but suddenly wondering if she'd ever, ever in a million years be in the pages of *Vogue*. The possibility lit up in front of her like a star falling to earth.

'Oh, I can't believe it. You're thinking about it now,' Lily snapped, 'aren't you?'

'No,' May said, horrified at being caught out. 'No, of course I'm not.'

'I warned you this might happen, didn't I?' Lily said sternly. 'You're addicted. You've been corrupted. All the attention has gone to your head and you've lost your heart. You've forgotten that you started all this to fulfil yourself and then to help people. Not to be a success. And now that's what matters most to you. You care too much for the least important thing at the expense of the *only* important thing.'

'No.' May paused as she took in Lily's words. 'I don't. Does it matter that I like the attention as long as I'm still helping people?

'Someone needs to save you from yourself before you sell your soul for a fantasy. Someone needs to love you more than they want you to love them.'

'What does that mean?' May frowned.

'That they'll have the guts to tell you the truth about what you're turning into, even if you'll hate them for it. You need an intervention,' Lily said. 'I'm just praying that boyfriend of yours grows a backbone – before it's too late.'

But Ben didn't dare tell May the truth any more. He was still holding out for the moments, late at night, when May forgot about her adoring fans and photo shoots, and just curled up to him and squeezed him tight. He still cherished the now few-and-far-between times they talked about absolutely nothing, just to connect. He kept the engagement ring in the drawer of his bedside table, hoping that one day soon all the attention would be enough for her and she wouldn't need it any more. He hoped that she still loved him enough to want him. He hoped she still knew herself enough to realise what was false and what was true.

And then came the announcement that finally broke the now fragile bond between them. Lily had only bought the American rights to May's book so her agent was free to sell it all over the world, a job in which she took enormous pleasure. The number of the countries slowly began to add up: France, Spain, Bulgaria, Russia, Brazil, China, Iceland, India, Japan… And May found it all incredibly thrilling, if mainly for the kudos rather than financial reward, which, with small advances, wasn't yet significant. Until the agent landed the coup of her career in a deal with an extremely prestigious publishing house in London. They wanted to publish *Men, Money and Chocolate* in just three months, in time for Christmas. They wanted the author to come over for at least a month for pre- and post-publicity. They wanted television appearances, book tours, magazine spreads, newspaper interviews... They offered May half a million pounds. She took it.

LOSS

May was packing. Three large suitcases lay on the bed, each half-filled with clothes, shoes, make-up, toiletries. Ben sat on the sofa in the living room, pretending to read the newspaper.

'It looks like you're going on vacation,' he said, without looking up.

'It's not a holiday,' May said, sighing, 'it's work. And I invited you to come. It wouldn't matter, it would be free. The publishing company is paying for everything.'

'Oh, it "wouldn't matter", would it? That really sounds like you want me to come,' Ben said. 'Well, excuse me, but I think I'll decline that heartfelt invitation. Anyway, you know I can't leave the shop.'

'Of course you can,' May snapped, annoyed at his lack of support or enthusiasm. 'It's not like we desperately need the money now, is it?'

'It's not about the money,' Ben said. 'Not everything is about money.' He knew of course he could go with her. Of course he could leave the shop. But that would be making it easier for her to go, and he was damned if he'd do that.

'Fine,' May said, not wanting to get into yet another fight about the merits of money. She stuffed another three dresses into a suitcase, along with two pairs of jeans. One could never predict the English weather so it was always best to prepare for every eventuality. She glanced over at Ben, still hiding behind his newspaper. She tried to let it go, but, still convinced she was right, she couldn't.

'I don't know why you're acting as if this bloody brilliant book deal is, like, the worst thing that ever happened to us.' May sighed. 'Hell, I thought you'd be happy, I thought you'd at least be proud of me.'

Ben looked up. 'Careful, it sounds like you're turning into an American. You might just have to come back.'

'What?' May frowned. 'Of course I'm coming back. What the hell – what are you talking about?'

'Nothing.'

'It's *not* nothing.' May held another dress in mid-air. 'You think I'm not coming back?'

Ben shrugged. And for a moment, in the silence, she sensed him. Hurt. Scared. Alone. Her heart twisted in her chest and the only thing she wanted right then was to run to the sofa, hold Ben tight, tell him how much she loved him, promise him that everything was going to be okay.

'Of course I'm coming back,' May said softly. 'How could you think –'

'I never know what you're gonna do,' Ben cut in. 'You just do whatever you want; you don't tell me.'

May dropped the dress into the suitcase and suddenly, at his words, the distance between the bed and the sofa seemed infinite. He'd poked at her again and any sympathy she'd had evaporated in a puff of hurt. She felt her hackles rise, all the sharper because what he'd said was true.

'That's rubbish,' May retorted, 'and you're being a baby. I'm doing this for us. With this money we can pay off the mortgage and all our debts; we can even buy another bookshop if you want.'

'Well, I don't want,' Ben said, aware that right now he did sound like a baby. 'I'm perfectly happy with this one. I don't want to be the CEO of some chain of stupid corporate bookshops. I like being with the customers. I like connecting with people. You used to like it too, before you became better than everyone else – too important to bother with the likes of me.'

May glared at him, not knowing how to best defend herself from the accusation. 'Well,' she snapped, 'if that's the way you feel then maybe I won't come back after all.' Though, of course, she didn't mean it.

'Good,' Ben said. 'Maybe you shouldn't.' Though, of course, he didn't mean it either. But, once it was said, both of them felt so hurt and angry that neither wanted to be the first to take it back.

Ben sat at the far end of the bar. He hated bars. They were loud and lascivious and, while they no longer stank of smoke, he swore he could always smell the faintest whiff of desperation and despair hanging in the air whenever he was dragged into one. But this time Ben didn't care. The fight with May had been so bad that a black coffee at Alice's café just wouldn't cut it now. He'd ordered a scotch neat and was currently coughing his way through it.

Ben didn't notice her at first, the tall thin blonde sitting at the other end of the bar. He didn't notice anyone or anything, except the bottom of his glass. He was going to lose May; he knew it. It was over. She would go to England and she wouldn't come back. She'd probably meet some rich, successful author at an event and shack up with him. After all, why wouldn't she? Now she was rich and successful herself and clearly fed up with him, what was keeping her here?

Ben sighed, gulped down the last of his scotch and ordered another. The blonde smiled at him, trying to catch his eye. Ben nodded slightly, then returned to his drink. The blonde, interpreting the nod as an invitation instead a dismissal, stepped off her stool and strode across to him. She stuck her thin arm in front of Ben's glass so he had to look up, then flashed him a perfect set of bright white teeth and stroked his shoulder.

'Is this seat taken?' she asked, sliding into it before he could say anything. 'I'm Nina, by the way. It's lovely to meet ya.' She turned to the barman, slowly wrapping her long manicured fingers around the stem of her cocktail glass. 'Raspberry cosmo again, Ryan, thank you, darlin'.'

'I'm not looking for company, Mina,' Ben said without looking up. 'I'm married. Well, actually I'm not, but I damn well should be.'

'It's Nina,' she drawled, 'and what on earth is that supposed to mean?'

Ben shrugged.

'So you married or not?' Nina persisted. ''Cause you ain't wearing a ring.'

'I am in my heart. But no, I'm not married,' Ben admitted, 'not technically.'

Nina threw her head back and laughed, loud and long, as though he'd said something absolutely hilarious. 'Well, if you ain't yanking my chain, 'cause that's the first time I ever heard a man say that. Usually it's the other way round.' She slid her hand onto Ben's thigh. 'In which case y'all won't mind my doing this.'

'Yes,' Ben said firmly and removing her hand, 'I'm afraid I do. Only my… May can touch me like that.'

'Aw, that's a shame. Now, what d'ya say your name was, sweetie?'

'I didn't.' Ben downed his scotch in one gulp and then signalled for another.

'No need fer names anyway,' Nina said, giving Ben a wink. 'Always better that way.'

Ben sighed, ignored her and kept drinking. If only May was with him. If only she wasn't about to leave and take his heart with her. What had gone so wrong between them? He couldn't understand. What had he done? What had he not done? Why hadn't he been able to save their relationship? Ben put his head between his hands and groaned. His eyes were glazing over; his memory was beginning to fade, his senses starting to numb. That was good. He ordered another drink.

The next time Nina slipped her hand onto his thigh Ben didn't move it off. If he was honest, it felt good to experience a little affection, a little comfort after all he'd been through. He couldn't remember the last time he and May had made love. He couldn't remember the last time she'd looked at him the way she'd used to. He would give anything, absolutely anything, to have that back. But he knew he couldn't. So he'd have to make do with what he had right now. Compared to the love of his life, the woman sitting next to him was small compensation, but at least she soothed his broken spirit just a little bit. And, after all Ben had been through in the past year, his alcohol-addled brain decided he surely deserved that much.

He turned to Nina. 'My girlfriend is leaving me.'

'Aw, I'm sorry, darlin',' Nina purred, though she didn't seem sorry at all.

'I don't know…' Ben's mind was starting to spin as he tried to find the right words. 'I don't know what went wrong, what I did so wrong.'

'Petal,' Nina said softly, sliding her hand further up his thigh, 'love is like this: if someone wants ya, ya can't do it wrong enough to put 'em off, but if they don't, then ya can't do it right enough to convince 'em to stay. Trust me, I've tried it both ways, been through a *lot* of men in the process, but that's the truth of it, believe me.'

And as Ben caught the lost look in her eye, he did. It made sense. Here he was twisting himself into knots, hurting his brain and breaking his heart, to try to get May to love him again. But it was no use. He couldn't do it right enough. She didn't want him any more; that much was clear. And Ben could barely breathe from the pain of accepting it.

'I know you're hurtin', sweetie.' Nina leant close to whisper into Ben's ear. The heat of her breath brushed his skin and he shivered. 'But I know just how to take that pain away. It's my special gift, my magic…'

Ben let his gaze drop down to the V-neck of her low-cut dress, to the dip between her breasts. When Ben first met May he'd known that was it as far as he and other women were concerned. When they'd first made love, he knew he never wanted to see another woman naked. And that hadn't changed. Even now, he was so uninterested in this woman that he could barely be bothered to respond.

But the despair and desperation he'd felt in the air when he'd walked into the bar had now sunk deep into his skin and he'd do anything to shift it. This woman was like alcohol or cocaine. She was offering him a drug that would lift him up out of his pit. And, with five shots of whisky firing through his blood and a bad case of unrequited love weighing down his heart, Ben didn't see why he shouldn't take it.

When Ben crept back into his flat at half past three that morning, May was fast asleep and surrounded by suitcases. He switched on a table light and tiptoed over to watch while she slept for what he figured was probably the last time. He leant forward, intending to kiss May's forehead, to pretend that he'd get to spend the rest of his life loving her, to forget everything that had happened since he'd walked out. But then another wave of nausea passed through him, so he staggered towards the sofa, sat down and promptly passed out.

Ben woke early to May clattering around in the kitchen. He groaned, slowly opening his eyes and squinting in the sunshine. The bright light stung so he shut his eyes again. A few minutes later Ben tried to sit up, but his head throbbed and spun, and he was hit by another wave of nausea.

'May,' he said weakly.

'What?' she called, her voice still frosty, though she'd been loud on purpose, hoping to wake him so they might make up without her having to make the first move.

'What time is it?'

'Ten past six. I've got half an hour. The limo driver's already waiting outside with my stuff. I didn't know whether or not to wake you,' May lied, desperately hoping that Ben still loved her but too scared to ask, desperately hoping that they could reconcile before she left but too scared to beg. 'You seemed pretty out of it.'

Ben's stomach twisted so tightly he thought he'd throw up right there. But he knew this time the sickness had nothing to do with alcohol. She was going to leave him without saying goodbye. She really didn't love him any more. With great difficulty Ben pulled himself off the sofa and walked into the kitchen. He slid onto a stool next to the coffee machine.

'Want some?' May picked up a cup.

Ben shook his head.

'I'll call you tonight, from the hotel, or whenever I can, okay?' Her tone was dismissive, and for Ben, having no idea how she really felt, it was as though each word cut into his skin. 'But I don't know what they've got planned for me when I get there,' May continued.

When he looked at her Ben felt as though he was seeing May from a thousand miles away, from beneath the sea or through thick fog. Her voice was cold and crisp, her body stiff, her eyes empty, as though her soul had left ahead of her and was already halfway across the ocean.

'You've already gone,' Ben said. 'You left a long time ago.'

May bit her lip. Having forgotten what Rose had said, she still thought true love should be easy, but her heart was hurting as though it was about to crack open in her chest. She could hardly bear it. Suddenly May just wanted the pain to stop. She wanted to run away until it was all better and then she'd come back. She blinked back tears and glanced towards the door. Ben watched her, seeing in her eyes how much she wanted to leave. And so he decided to say the thing that would let her off the hook.

'May,' Ben said, unable to look her in the eye. 'Last night I… I slept with someone else.'

For several moments time slowed down as it had when her mother had died, and May just stared at him. She had no words. There were no words. She looked at Ben, waiting for him to take it back, to undo it, to say it wasn't true. But he said nothing. He gazed at her, tears in his eyes. She waited a moment longer. Then she ran. And Ben, his heart now broken in two, watched her go.

DENIAL

$\mathbf{M}$ay didn't call Ben when she reached the hotel as she'd promised to do. Instead she sat on the bed and stared out of the window until, at some point in the early hours of the morning, she finally fell asleep. And when she woke up her head ached as though she hadn't slept at all. She glanced at the alarm clock on the bedside table. She'd been unconscious for twelve hours. Afternoon sunlight streamed in through the windows: floor-to-ceiling glass with long cream silk curtains still pulled back. May blinked up at the tasteful glass chandelier, then glanced around the rest of the room: plush, deep pile carpets, flowered silk-upholstered sofa, white dressing table and chairs, a writing desk that stood by another window that overlooked Hyde Park. The hotel was exquisite, expensive – swanky, that's what Ben would have called it.

May rubbed her temples. Slowly she got up and walked across the carpet to the bathroom: marble tiles, heated floors, a bathtub that would fit a family of four. She stood in front of the mirror, pulled her mess of tangled hair away from her face and gazed into her own shining eyes: the colour of moss after rain. She swallowed hard, trying to blink back tears and practise a fake smile, wide and bright, so no one would see that her heart was broken inside her chest.

That evening her prestigious London publishers took her out to dinner. She arrived twenty minutes early, surrendered her coat, then sat down at the empty table for five. She ordered a bottle of water and gingerly fingered the silver cutlery. She watched the waiters gliding between the tables with trays and plates held elegantly aloft as though they were performers in an intricate modern dance routine.

May glanced around at the impeccably dressed people populating the booths close to her. She sat up a little straighter. Only a few metres away sat the star of a film she'd watched on the plane: in the flesh, actually eating real food with a knife and fork. Next to him was someone else she recognised, though it took May a few minutes to place her. It was Caitlyn Walker. A bestselling author: tall, thin, blonde, beautiful... an American writer who'd had seven of her books turned into multi-million-dollar films, every one of which was a box-office smash. Little did May know that Ms Walker was far more lost even than May, suffering from a broken heart, a battered spirit, a wounded soul, and writer's block.

On the surface at least, the evening went wonderfully. May's publishers loved her, loved the book and were very excited about the high-octane itinerary they'd lined up for the coming month. Almost every hour was accounted for, with only a half-day off on Sundays. They'd booked her appearances on every chat show, daytime and evening, fluffy and cultural. They'd appointed interviews in newspapers – tabloids and broadsheets – and magazines. They'd arranged advance book readings around London, followed by a nationwide tour once the book came out. It was BIG. And it was only the beginning.

When May finally returned to the hotel, it was long past midnight and her head was spinning so much she had to hold onto the wall while opening the door to her room. She walked over to the sofa and sat back with a sigh, still dizzy and staring up at the ceiling, breathing deeply, trying to steady herself, trying to figure out what she was feeling. And then, slowly, she knew. Right now, finally alone again, she didn't feel happy or excited or scared or sad. She was numb; she felt nothing, absolutely nothing at all, which was the worst thing of all. Just as Lily had warned, she'd lost her heart by focusing on success instead of self-fulfilment, and with it the love of her life.

'That's quite a story,' the interviewer gushed. 'You must feel pretty damn proud of yourself, what with all you've achieved?'

May was sitting on the sofa of her Hyde Park hotel room with a tabloid journalist. They'd done the photo shoot earlier that day and it had been a little risqué. She knew Ben wouldn't have approved. But of course, sadly, it didn't matter what he thought any more.

'I don't know, I suppose I feel, well…'

'So, what'll the headline be?' the journalist mused, biting his pencil. 'From penniless waitress to international writer –'

'Well, I wasn't really a waitress. I owned the café.'

'Okay,' he considered, 'from baker to bestseller –'

'Well, actually I wasn't –'

'Yep, that's not bad. 'Course we need to sex it up a little, but I'm sure the editor'll take care of that, smarmy git. So,' he said, turning back to her, 'how *do* you feel, now you've done everything you've ever dreamed of?'

It was an easy question, with an easy answer. May opened her mouth, waiting for all the clichés about living a fairy-tale life to trip off her tongue. But nothing came out. She was silent.

Surprised to be still waiting, the journalist prompted her. 'Stupid question I suppose. So then, is there anything left, anything else you still want to achieve, or would you say you have it all?'

What else did she want? May pondered this. Well, to go back in time and make different choices. To have her life back, her lovely little life before she lost her heart and all sense of perspective. To know unconditional love again. To have joy in her heart and peace in her soul. To be a good person again, a worthwhile person, a person who brings light to other people's lives. To remember why she promoted the book in the first place. And to feel something. Anything at all.

'No, nothing else,' May answered, smiling. 'I have everything I've ever wanted.'

'Yeah?' The journalist laughed. 'And everything every other bugger in the world wants too!'

'Yes.' May nodded. 'Yes, I'm very lucky, very lucky indeed.'

It was May's first half-day off. The first morning she hadn't crawled out of bed at the crack of dawn, the first time she'd had more than a minute to herself. And now it was almost midday and she hadn't got out of bed at all. She'd turned the television on and off again numerous times, tried reading the papers, but nothing could hold her attention. Every few seconds she glanced at the telephone by the bed. A soft voice inside her heart whispered to her, telling her to call Ben. And her cousin, Faith. Now May knew why she was so scared to call Ben, but didn't really understand why she was putting off calling her favourite cousin. Faith would be rather hurt if she knew. May told herself she'd been meaning to every day and couldn't understand why she kept putting it off. Sometimes, when she'd escaped the media madness for a moment or two and was walking through the park, or had stopped to listen to a street musician, or given a homeless person a ten-pound note – since meeting Harry she'd sought them out – May thought of Faith and her heart ached from missing her. But she was nervous too. Probably because she knew that Faith would say it was all her fault that everything had gone wrong. And she didn't want to hear that because she knew it was.

Another week passed in the blink of an eye. The month was almost up and May still hadn't called Faith or Ben. But most of the time she didn't have to think about it or what to do next because every decision was made for her. And that, at least, was a blessing.

Now she sat in the back of a taxi, speeding towards her very first UK book signing. It was being held in a famous bookshop on Oxford Street, the name of which had momentarily escaped her, the importance of which had not. It was an incredibly prestigious location to have as the first stop on her book tour and, as such, she should have been feeling extremely excited and certainly very proud. But May felt neither of these things; she didn't even feel nervous, just numb. As usual.

As the taxi swept up to the venue, May was surprised to see the queue of customers snaking out of the bookshop and down the street. And she was even more surprised when they clapped and cheered as she walked inside. But the biggest surprise of all was saved for when May sat at the table and looked up to see the first person waiting for her, book in hand and grinning from ear to ear.

Jake.

She blinked at him, unable to believe it. Even looking straight at him: tall and broad, blond hair and blue eyes… Absolutely completely and utterly gorgeous – and he still knew it. The man who had adored her for a few brief blissful months, then left her six months after she'd become needy and clingy and ever-so-slightly obsessed. The man for whom she had given up her sense of self, the reason she had vowed never to do it again. Indeed the man who was a major reason why she'd screwed things up so spectacularly with Ben.

May had fantasised about this moment for years. Since the day he'd walked out, since she'd self-published her book, she dreamt that one day it might become a bestseller and Jake would see it in a window.

He would read it and realise he'd made a hideous, horrible mistake. He'd see how much everyone else adored and admired her, and he'd come running. Just as she still wished her father would.

And now here he was, standing three feet in front of her. She stared at him. He stepped forward, holding her book, smiling the dazzling smile that had always made her melt. In the next few seconds the last few months of their relationship flashed through her mind: the nights when she'd crept out of bed, reading his phone messages in the dark, finding nothing but new depths of self-loathing and despair she never imagined she'd reach. The days she'd pursued him, calling far too often, trying to spice things up, to delve deeper into him, chasing him – the more he pulled away until he started being cruel. Staying close to him no matter what he did or how much it hurt. Until finally, he left her.

May's breath caught in her throat and, unable to speak, she waited to see what Jake would do next.

'Hi,' he said, still grinning. 'I'm hoping you might sign my book.'

'Yes of course.' May composed herself and held his gaze. 'Do you want a dedication?'

'Please.'

'Name?'

'Oh, don't tell me I meant so little to you, Maya. It'd break my heart.'

May took the book from him and scribbled his name. Silky smooth words still tripped off his tongue so easily, as seductive as chocolate caramels. She shivered a little. *I thought,* she wanted to say, *that it was I who meant so little to* you.

'It's May now,' she said. 'I go by May.'

'Oh,' he said, 'but on your book —'

'Well, to my friends.' She handed him back the book, and Jake took it as though she'd just given him the crown jewels.

'Thank you,' he said softly, 'for still calling me your friend.'

May gave a slight shrug, glancing towards the long queue of people behind him, some of them looking pointedly at their watches and glaring at Jake for making them wait.

'Well,' she said, 'I guess I'd better get on.'

Jake nodded. 'Yeah, right, of course. But, please, let me take you out for dinner tonight. If you don't have plans, fabulous famous person that you are now. Or if you do, break them.' And there was that smile again. The one that seemed to reach right down into May's chest and tug at her heart. She hadn't seen him for so long, hadn't loved him for even longer, but his smile still had that effect on her. May willed herself to say no, to lie, to dismiss him, to say she never wanted to see him again.

But instead she said, 'Okay, when I'm done here, why don't I meet you at the bar across the street?'

Jake nodded again, flashed her one last smile and was gone.

May didn't like bars, but she knew Jake did. And she supposed it was better than the intimacy of a restaurant booth or, worse still, her hotel room. When she first walked inside she couldn't see him. She'd been half hoping he wouldn't be there, but, now that he wasn't, the disappointment quickened her pulse, the familiar sense of rejection tasted like copper in her mouth. She turned to go.

'Maya, May, wait!'

She glanced back to see Jake hurrying towards her, two glasses of wine held aloft: one white, one red. He handed May the red as he reached her.

'Cabernet sauvignon.'

Despite herself, May smiled. 'You remembered.'

'But, of course.' He flashed his bright white teeth at her again.

Jake led the way to the back of the bar and May followed, like a magnet, sliding into a booth before she could think to object. Their knees touched under the table and she shifted slightly so it wouldn't happen again. She thought of Ben at home, oblivious. Then she remembered what he'd done. So, technically, it didn't matter what she did now; she'd only be evening the score.

'I can't believe you're really here,' Jake said, smiling at her.

'No. Me neither.'

'And what's happened to you since… I mean, it's quite incredible.'

'What?' May asked. 'My evolution from a pathetic mess into –'

'Hey, I never thought you were a pathetic mess,' Jake said. 'At least, not at first. But when you got all those rejections, I suppose you lost yourself for a little while. I bet those agents and publishers are kicking themselves now, right?'

'I doubt it.' May shrugged. 'I don't think I'm that big a deal.'

'Well, judging by what I read in the papers, you're the only one who doesn't.' He looked at her and held her gaze until May looked away. 'Do I make you nervous?'

'You make me doubt myself,' May said quietly. Perhaps it was because she was so much weaker now, whittled away by all she'd won and lost, hollowed out by too much desperation and desire, but May felt herself regressing in Jake's presence, becoming who she'd been all those years ago: needy, lonely, looking for love outside herself.

'I remember what you liked about me back then and what you didn't,' May added. 'And I don't think you'll like me right now.'

'You're wrong.' Jake reached up and ran his fingertip slowly along her cheek to her chin. 'I find you incredibly attractive right now.'

May sighed softly. 'Don't.'

Then he kissed her. Jake's lips were warm, soft and just slightly wet. May was surprised she remembered how he'd tasted. It felt comforting, just the way chocolate cake had made her feel when she was empty and alone. As Jake slid his hands down her back, she knew how easy it would be to take it all the way. What a relief it would be, what a nice way to numb the pain rising up inside her belly. But then something shocking happened. In the darkness of that moment, May suddenly understood why Ben had done what he'd done. She could feel his heart as strongly as she now felt her own: so lost and loveless that she'd search anywhere to make it feel again.

But this wasn't how she wanted to do it. It hadn't worked with chocolate, and it wouldn't work with sex. And, as Jake lightly trailed a finger across her breasts, a small voice inside her spoke up. *No*, it whispered. *No.* So softly she almost couldn't hear it. *No.* Without thinking, May jumped up, almost spilling her wine over Jake. She apologised profusely, ran through the tables, out of the bar and jumped into the first taxi she saw.

Half an hour later, back in her hotel room, May sat on the edge of the bed. She was no longer numb. She was so filled with conflicting emotions that she couldn't for the life of her fathom how she actually felt: sad, lonely, guilty, sorry, angry, scared... She didn't know what to do. Suddenly she missed her mother; she missed Ben, Lily and Faith. The longing seized her at her throat, and the anger at herself for everything she'd done pumped through her veins. She wanted to thump the walls and wail, smash all the mirrors and rip the curtains to shreds. But she didn't even have the energy to get off the bed.

And then, for the first time in a very long time, May started to cry. For all the mistakes she'd made, for all the decisions she wished she could undo, for all the pain she'd caused.

For all she had loved, and all she had lost.

FAITH

When May awoke the first – and only – thing she wanted to do was call Ben. But it was still only two o'clock in the morning for him and she worried about how he might react. After pondering for a moment or two, she picked up the phone and called Faith. Her cousin answered at the second ring.

'Hello?'

'Hi, I, um, it's…' May scrambled for a suitable apology for not having called in fifteen months, wishing she'd prepared something.

'Oh, May, how wonderful!' Faith exclaimed. 'How are you, lovely?'

A wave of relief washed over May; clearly her cousin still never held grudges.

'I'm so, so sorry I didn't call,' May said. 'I, well, for the last fifteen months I… I lost all sense of myself, and everything that really mattered, and I just…'

'It's okay,' Faith said soothingly. 'I signed up to the newsletter on your website. It was very informative.' May could sense Faith smiling. 'And I just Googled you whenever I wanted to see your face. So it's all good.'

'Oh no.' May sighed, absolutely mortified. 'I – I was pretty, incredibly busy. But, of course, that's not the point at all.'

'Don't worry. I know. I know you were,' Faith said. 'And I knew you were going through some sort of identity crisis too. I expected it.'

'You did?' May frowned, sinking back into the plush silk pillows on her bed, feeling the tension in her body begin to subside at the sound of her cousin's voice.

'Of course,' Faith said, 'you got sucked into the world of Comparison, Control and Crazy. It was only to be expected.'

'You know about that?' May asked, stunned. 'How on earth do you know about that?'

'Oh, it's quite common knowledge among us esoteric types,' Faith said breezily. 'It's a very typical stage in a person's development if they step into the public eye, and a very challenging one at that. Some people get stuck in that stage for the rest of their lives.'

'What stage?' May asked, a little lost.

'The stage of seeking,' Faith explained. 'The stage of longing, yearning, wanting... The stage of thinking that "it" – happiness, contentment and joy – is always around the corner with the next big thing: promotion, holiday, car, house, mansion, magazine cover...'

'But –' May hugged a cushion to her chest, absently twisting its tassels round her fingers – 'I thought

I'd been through that stage before when I was obsessed with finding a man, money and weight-loss, remember?'

'Ah, but that was different,' Faith said, 'that was when you had nothing. And now you have everything. It's a whole new ball game.' She laughed. 'Did you like my American metaphor? I threw it in to make you feel more at home.' She giggled again and May felt the warmth of Faith's laugh like a balm on her soul, soothing her wounded spirit.

'Oh, Fay, I've missed you so much.' May let out a heavy sigh. 'I want to see you, I need to see you. Are you free?'

'For you? Of course I am, but are *you*?'

'No,' May said, 'but I will be.'

Faith and May walked slowly along the river, arm in arm. Her cousin looked exactly as May remembered: her long wild black hair, crazily colourful clothes – this time a pair of purple leggings, a red tutu and a bright green jumper – and the most beautiful smile she'd ever seen. The late-afternoon sun shone softly through the trees, shimmering on the water. May sighed happily and, suddenly overcome with an inexplicable rush of love and joy, squeezed her cousin tightly. Faith squeezed her back.

'Did they make a fuss?'

'Not really,' May said. 'I told them I was having some sort of artistic breakdown and I needed a few days off. I expect they're used to it, all those dramatic, diva artists they have to deal with. They didn't try to stop me.'

The two women walked along in silence for a while, hearing only the occasional quack or splash of a duck landing on the river. A light wind blew through the trees, rustling the leaves, and every now and then a cyclist passed them on the path. May really wanted to talk, to get her cousin's advice on every crazy thing she'd done over the last few months, but she couldn't bring herself to break the silence. It had been so long since she'd heard it: the thick syrupy softness of the air, so still it almost sat on her skin and May wanted to soak in it for as long as she could.

When at last they reached the end of the path and began to stroll across the fields in the direction of Faith's flat, May spoke up. 'So tell me more about the ball game.'

'What? Oh, yes, okay then,' Faith said, taking a moment or two to remember what she'd been talking about. 'Yes, so... the stage of striving for everything, seeking happiness, seeing it in the distance but never feeling it inside.'

'Exactly,' May said. 'That one, 'cause I thought I'd been through that, dealt with it. I mean, I spent my whole life striving to find happiness in something, but when I let go of everything, when I found myself, when I stood at the top of that mountain in Arizona... Then I knew I'd found happiness *inside* me; I knew it wasn't out there. I stopped striving. I found peace. And then I went and bloody well lost it all again.'

'Ah, but you see,' Faith said, smiling, 'it's quite easy to find peace on a mountain top, away from the world – all the advertisements, TV, magazines, rich and famous people, the constant invitations to compare yourself to others and find yourself wanting – all alone, where you can feel the calm even in the air. But to stand right in the middle of all the madness in this crazy world and still be at peace? Now that takes real strength of self.'

May sighed 'Ah, well then, I supposed I never had that.'

'Hey.' Faith squeezed her hand. 'Don't feel bad about it, most people don't. So when they get dropped into the illusory world of fame and fortune, they lose their heads and, more important still, their hearts. They compare themselves to everyone else. They become convinced they have to keep striving for more and more. They have no perspective. They can't let go – of money or work and the need to have control over everything. So they have no peace. And that's when the craziness sets in.'

'Yes.' May giggled, suddenly seeing herself so clearly. 'That's exactly what happened to me.'

'Exactly, it could have happened to anyone.'

'Not you.'

'Well, no.' Faith smiled. 'Not me, but then I am a saint.'

At this May giggled louder until they were both laughing and couldn't stop. Faith fell onto the grass, rolling around in her tutu, and May flopped down beside her.

'Oh, oh, oh,' May exclaimed breathlessly, 'that was my life, that was me. I can't believe it, you've just... it's like you were watching me the whole time.'

'Sometimes I know you even better than you know yourself.' Faith giggled, still catching her breath.

'True, that's true, that's so true,' May realised, 'I'm only just starting to see it, how deluded I've been, driven by the little gremlin inside me, desperate to get his grubby little hands on all the world has to offer, without caring a damn for the consequences. I've been ignoring the whispers of my heart, telling me how miserable I was making myself' – with a stab in her chest, May thought of Ben – 'and everyone else.'

'Forgive yourself for that,' Faith said softly, echoing Harry. She sat up and pulled May's hands into her lap. 'There really aren't many people strong enough to resist the pull of illusion: of fabulous shoes and fancy dresses, mansions and magazine covers, the attention and adoration of strangers. People are pulled in by the sparkle, mistaking the rush of glitz and glamour for true joy. It's too easy to become trapped in the cycle of celebrity, succeeding and striving, while deep down wondering why you don't feel as satisfied as you should and why true happiness always evades you.'

May couldn't do anything but nod. She was lost for words. She pulled Faith into a hug and buried her face in her cousin's hair. It smelt of patchouli oil. Together they toppled over and rolled around on the grass, laughing until May began to cry. Faith lay still and held her cousin, with May's head snuggled in the nook of her arm while May sobbed. Faith stroked May's long dark curls and soft white skin, and kept smiling, because she knew what May didn't yet: that this was the beginning of everything, and everything was going to be all right. In fact it would be wonderful.

Eventually May sat up, wiping her eyes and sighing softly. 'But why did it all go so wrong? Why did I mess up my life so much, why did I do it? I thought, I mean… when I got to America I read all these books, about creating my dreams, and I believed them. And I thought when I finally got all I ever wanted, it'd make me happy. But now I think I didn't really have a clue what I wanted, 'cause it certainly didn't make me happy… in fact I only made myself even more miserable than I was when I had nothing.'

Faith lifted a finger to wipe a tear from May's cheek. 'The problem with getting what you want is many of your desires come from the gremlin inside. It's all about striving, wanting to be better and have more. Not realising how wonderful you already are, not appreciating the magic in what you already have.'

May nodded, hiccupping. 'That's the really crazy thing. I *was* happy, so happy, at the beginning of all this. Then I started to think it wasn't enough, I started wanting more… and I tumbled downhill from there.'

'Well,' Faith said abruptly, smiling and jumping up, 'now you're at the bottom again it's time to start climbing up. But this time pick a different hill. One that gives you what you need to be happy, not what you *think* you want.' She reached out her hands to May, who grasped them and pulled herself up.

Faith laughed. 'There, you see. It's not so hard. You just need a little help from those who love you. And tell you the truth.'

The following morning May was snuggled on Faith's sofa, drinking rosehip tea. Her cousin was doing made-up yoga moves on the carpet, dressed in bright yellow satin pyjamas, giggling as she fell over her own feet.

'Oh, God, it feels so good to do absolutely nothing at all.' May sighed. 'I can't remember the last time

I wasn't doing, planning, plotting and thinking, all the time thinking…'

'Wouldn't it be cool if everyone spent at least half an hour a day doing absolutely nothing at all?' Faith grinned, poking her nose out between her legs. 'It's such a wonderful thing for creating peace and perspective, and for helping people realise that who they are matters just as much, if not more, than what they do.'

'Sounds good to me.'

'And I mean absolutely *nothing*, not meditating or yoga or reading a good book, but nothing. Of course it helps to be in a pretty place, gazing out into nature. But even sitting in a chair staring at a wall will do.'

'Why absolutely nothing?' May asked. 'Surely relaxing activities are just as nurturing to your soul?'

'Well, I'm not saying those things aren't good too,' Faith said, twisting herself upside down so she was bent over double and May could no longer see her face behind a curtain of dark hair, 'but they're still somewhere in the realm of achieving something. When you do absolutely *nothing* at all, you're reminding yourself that life is short, that nothing you do is going to make you live any longer than you will, or make you a better person than you are, so you might as well stop and enjoy it before it goes by.'

'Yeah, I suppose it's ridiculous really,' May said. 'All that time I was trying to make my life better, I never even really enjoyed the betterness of it.'

Faith unwrapped herself and joined May on the sofa, stretching out like a cat. 'Ah, that was lovely.' She gave a satisfying sigh. 'Now I just need some sex.'

May laughed. 'How do you do it? Stay so calm and centred in all this craziness? How do you keep your peace and perspective? Because I'm a little scared that as soon as I step back into the madness of life I'm going to mess it all up again.'

'Oh, I don't know,' Faith said. 'It's a life-long journey. You can't put pressure on yourself to get it right the first, second or even fifth time. Simply try to balance your spiritual side with your material side as best you can. And remember that what your material side wants is usually not at all the same as what your spiritual side needs and, when in doubt, always tip the balance in favour of the latter. Then everything else will take care of itself.'

May sipped the last of her tea. 'I think I'll get that tattooed on my fingers so I never forget.'

'And some foundations,' Faith said. 'Get yourself some solid spiritual foundations. Then when the fame and fortune stuff tries to seduce you, when illusory promises of a fairy-tale life are waved in front of you, you'll find it much easier to keep hold of your spirit and soul, and to stop your heart from being stomped on.'

'Yes.' May smiled. 'I'd like to avoid being stomped on, if I can. So what are these foundations? Tell me, I need new material for my next book and, of course, my tattoos.'

Faith laughed at her cousin's question. 'Oh, but I don't know what yours are. I only know mine. I think they're unique to each of us. We just have to find them.'

'And where do we look?'

'Life gives you clues,' Faith said. 'You'll notice them if you're paying attention. Look around you, and listen to what people say. Not just when you've asked their advice, but often when it seems like they're saying nothing at all. I get the most wonderful insights from checkout girls.'

'Yes, you would.' May laughed. 'Lily told me something lovely a few months ago, a quote about asking life what it wants from me, instead of only asking for what I want from life.'

'Aunt Lily?' Faith's eyes widened with delight to hear of a ghost giving advice. 'How exciting!'

'No, sorry,' May said, laughing, 'it's another Lily, my American publisher. Although she did start to become a bit of a mum to me, actually, until I started ignoring her.'

'I'm sure she'll forgive you.'

'Not everyone is as able to do that as easily as you.' May thought of Ben and her heart contracted again. 'And I don't know they should.'

'Oh, May, stop punishing yourself so much. We all make mistakes. We're supposed to. It's part of being human; we can't learn without them. You've got to live, and bleed, and get your heart broken. There's no other way. After all, would you have believed me if I'd told you last year that getting your book published could – if you weren't very careful – make you more miserable than happy?'

'No,' May admitted. 'I don't suppose I would.'

'So, please, let it go. Let yourself off the hook, get back to your life, but this time forget about what your gremlin wants,' Faith said, 'and instead ask your heart what you need.'

But May didn't have to ask. She already knew. She felt it in her heart, body, blood and bones. 'I need to go home.'

TRUTH

The next day May returned to London. She met with her publishers again and told them that she needed to leave as soon as she'd fulfilled her obligations. Which meant ten days, in ten different cities. She wanted to jump on the next plane to San Francisco but needed to keep her word, so she stayed grounded and did her best to give her readings with gusto, respond with long, thoughtful answers to all her Q&As and chat with customers as she signed their books. And because May focused on taking care of those around her, instead of caring only about what she wanted, the ten days passed quickly and before she knew it she was flying home.

By the time May stood again on the corner of her San Francisco street, she half-wished she'd waited a little longer. She didn't know what to do or say to Ben. She paced up and down the spot where the taxi had dropped her, hoping inspiration and courage would come, but it didn't. Eventually she gave up and walked to the bookshop, put her suitcases on the pavement and peered through the window.

Ben was there, in the back, unpacking books and stacking them in little piles on the desk. Her heart hurt at the sight of him. The hands that had held her so tightly, the lips that had kissed her, the arms that had lifted her, the chest that she'd so often pressed her face against... May thought about everything they'd been through, the love and hate, the joy and pain. And she wished it had been different, wished that she hadn't lost herself – and him – in striving for illusions that meant nothing. And she wished he hadn't left her, body and soul, to sleep with someone else. But she knew there was no point; everything that had happened had happened, and all that mattered now was what would happen next.

May paused for a moment, then pushed open the door and stepped inside. As the bell tinkled, Ben looked up and froze. She walked slowly towards him, leaving her suitcases at the door.

'Hello.'

'Hi,' he said, still staring at her, still holding onto a book.

May waited to see what would happen next. She thought about forgiveness, about how far they'd both pushed those boundaries. But, although she wanted to turn and walk away, thinking it was all too much, too painful to go through, that it would be easier to start again with somebody new, May remembered what Rose had said about love, about how soulmates must bring out each other's most painful, unresolved issues so they can be healed. So there was no running away from this. If she ran now, she'd find herself back here again, years from now, with another man, not Ben. And she wanted it to be Ben; she wanted it always to be Ben.

'I – I…' May stepped towards him slightly, tears in her eyes. But before she could say anything else, Ben spoke.

'I didn't sleep with her.'

'What?' May frowned.

'I kissed her, I touched her, but I stopped.'

'I don't understand, you told me… you told me that you did.'

'I know. I think, I wanted to hurt you, I wanted to make you suffer, as much as I possibly could,' Ben said softly. 'I wanted to punish you, for leaving me, for everything… Hell, I wanted to sleep with her, just so I really could hurt you. I know that's unbelievably horrible, but… anyway, I just couldn't. I didn't want to touch her. She wasn't you and I just, I just couldn't…'

'Oh,' May gasped. 'Oh –'

'We were in a restroom, for god's sake,' Ben hurried on, desperate to get the truth out, 'and I looked at her, and it was disgusting, she was disgusting, I was disgusting… and I ran out. But I knew it was the one way I had left to hurt you. You didn't seem to care about anything any more, not about me anyway; you were so… indifferent. I thought… I don't know. I don't know what I was doing. I never, never felt so, so… When I thought you were leaving me, I didn't think my heart could hold so much pain.'

May walked towards him, sniffing, tears running down her cheeks. They stood a few feet from each other. Ben held the book against his chest like a shield.

'I *did* love you,' May said. 'I *do*. Then. Now. Always. I just… I was so lost inside another world, the insane, ridiculous world of illusions and gremlins and, anyway, I lost my heart. I couldn't feel anything any more, not love, or pain, or joy. I was numb to everything except wanting…'

'Not me,' Ben said. 'You wanted everything, but you didn't want me.'

'Oh, God, no, that's not true.' May blinked away her tears, trying to focus. 'I wanted what I didn't have. More fame, attention, adoration. More fortune, book sales, deals… But it wasn't real. I mean, my wanting wasn't real. I didn't *really* want all that, not in my heart and soul. The only problem was I'd completely lost touch with those parts of me, and all I could hear was my mind, telling me every minute of every day what I wanted, how much, how much more…'

Ben sighed a little, leaning against his desk and sitting down. 'I should have said something,' he said. 'I just let it happen. I saw it, but I didn't even try to help you.'

'Oh God, it's not your fault,' May exclaimed, 'not even a little bit, not at all. I wouldn't have listened. I'd probably just have yelled at you. Or ignored you, like I did with Lily.'

'No, you're wrong,' Ben said. 'I mean, I know you would have yelled and all that, but I was responsible too, for your well-being, for the state of our relationship. I let you down. I let you lose yourself and I didn't say anything. You were like a drunk, or a drug addict shooting up in front of me, and I just let you do it, because I didn't want to lose you.'

'Don't be silly,' May said. 'That's ridiculous.'

'Is it? Really? Remember what we agreed?' Ben asked. 'We agreed to tell each other the truth, to love each other enough to do that, to… what was it you told me once?'

May felt her heart contract again. 'That true love is when you love another person more than you want them to love you.'

'Right, exactly, so you tell them the truth. You tell them what they might not want to hear. You tell them what might make them hate you. But you do it to try to save them from themselves because, if you don't, they might just lose their way forever.'

'Yes.' May nodded. 'Yes.'

'But I didn't. I just thought about myself, the whole time,' Ben said, 'and I told myself I was just thinking of you, being generous with you, letting you get away with being self-obsessed for a little while, letting you be imperfect, loving you unconditionally −'

'And you were, and that was amazing of you. That's part of true love: loving the whole of someone, all their flaws, who they really are, not just the good stuff, not just who you want them to be.'

'Yes, I get that,' Ben said, putting his book down and running his finger along the edge of the desk, 'and it's right. But can't both be right at the same time? Can't you tell someone the truth about their behaviour while still loving them, in spite of it? Can't you be honest *and* loving? Can't you tell the truth about what you see, and do it with love, kindness, compassion... Surely unconditional love isn't about silence; it's about taking care of your beloved, to the very best of your ability.'

May took a few steps to the desk and sat down next to him. Very slowly, Ben reached out, took her hand and held it in his.

'I think people get confused,' Ben said. 'I know I was. They think unconditional love is letting someone be, without saying anything. But now I know that to truly love is to say something, without judging.'

'I'm not sure I... what do you mean?'

'I mean, you don't yell and scream about how selfish someone is; you don't blame them for their choices, or try to get them to feel bad. You just state the facts, as you see them, kindly and calmly, and let them decide what to do with it.'

'Well,' May said, 'that sounds pretty amazing. But I still don't know if I would have listened to you, even if you'd done that then. I think I was too lost' – she gave a little smile – 'too self-obsessed, to hear you.'

'Maybe,' Ben said, 'maybe not. But perhaps you underestimate yourself too. You ever think of that?'

'No.' May smiled at him. 'I didn't, but –'

Ben smiled back at her. 'Well, I believe that if we say something, anything, *truly* to help the other person, and our relationship with them, without any underlying anger, blame, criticism... then they'll be able to hear what we say, without getting defensive, without screaming denials and hating us for it, because they'll feel the love with which we'd said it, and they'd know that our intention is pure and true. Then, I think, it's possible to tell someone almost anything and they'll listen and look for the truth of it inside themselves.'

'Anything?' May was beaming now. 'Even when you're telling them that they're being selfish and self-obsessed?'

'Yes!' Ben laughed, pulling her into a hug. 'Even that. Although, not being judgemental, you wouldn't put it quite like that, would you?'

'True, true. So,' May went on, breathing in the smell of him, almost unable to believe they were holding each other again, 'where did all this amazing wisdom come from?'

'Hey, how do you know I didn't come up with it all by myself? You think I'm a duffball?'

'A duffball?' May laughed. 'What on earth's that?'

'I don't know, but it ain't someone smart.' Ben squeezed her. 'I've been chatting with Lily. She comes into the bookshop sometimes and we talk…'

'Lily?' May asked. 'Really?'

'Don't worry.' Ben looked at her with a twinkle in his eye. 'I didn't sleep with her.'

May raised an eyebrow.

'Well, maybe we just fooled around a little…'

'Not funny.'

'Sorry, too soon for jokes?'

'No,' May replied, smiling, 'I just thought you knew.'

'Knew what?'

'That Lily's a lesbian.' May giggled at the look of surprise on Ben's face. 'She's been with her lover, Megan, for over twenty years.'

'Ah,' Ben said, 'so that's why she was immune to my charms.'

May raised an eyebrow. 'Yeah, *that's* why.'

Ben laughed and kissed her. Warmth flushed May's skin and her lips tingled. 'I love you.'

'I love you too.'

'So, do you think we can do all that compassionate honesty stuff?' May asked. 'Do you think we've got what it takes?'

'Well, I think it's an essential ingredient to a happy relationship,' Ben said, 'and without it we'll end up floating apart, separating like... like butter and milk in a bad batch of pancake batter.'

May laughed. 'Okay, but why the bizarre cooking metaphor?'

'Shut up,' Ben retorted, tickling her. 'Because I'm starving, that's why. I haven't eaten in, like, ten hours.'

'Well then, I say we go upstairs,' May said, 'and eat.' She stood up, reaching out her hand to pull him up. 'What do you fancy?'

'Pancakes.'

'All right,' May said, 'but not those small and thick, weird American pancakes. The real ones: thin and crispy with lots of sugar and lemon.'

'Crêpes,' Ben said.

'You call them that,' May said, smiling, 'but to me they're plain old pancakes, just like my mum used to make.'

BIRTH

Ben and May strolled along the pebbled paths of the Japanese Tea Garden, hand in hand. The sun was setting slowly behind the trees and they walked in silence. It had been almost six months since May had come home and she felt better than ever before. They were applying compassionate honesty to their relationship and it was working wonderfully. It was perfect. Not completely calm and utterly unblemished, which is what May used to believe a perfect relationship should be, but much better than that. She discovered that a deeper, more profound perfection was to be found in forgiveness, empathy and compassion. With trust and truth, they began to heal many of the hurts they'd been carrying since childhood, just as Rose had promised they could. And May discovered that the old lady was right all along: love that stayed true in the presence of all your flaws was a much greater experience than love that was simply flawless.

And then Ben stopped walking.

'Hey.' May turned to him. 'What's up?'

'Why don't you want children?' Ben asked. 'I'm sorry, I keep telling myself not to ask, not to pressure you, but… please tell me.'

May looked at him. 'How do you know I don't?'

He shrugged. 'Things you've said. Things you haven't said. The way you reacted last time I asked.'

'Oh yes, that,' May remembered. 'Sorry about that. Well, it's just… I always thought I'd lose myself. I'd become a mother and I wouldn't know who I was any more. And I've always been just a little terrified that I'd mess up so completely my kids would need therapy till they died. That too.'

Ben laughed. 'Why on earth would you think that?'

'I supposed because I always thought I was a mess.' May shrugged. 'So, it stood to reason I'd be a mess as a mother.'

'You're not a mess.' Ben stroked a wisp of hair from her face. 'No more so than anyone else, anyway.'

May laughed and said, 'Oh well, that's all right then.' She looked at Ben, trying to think of another joke to lighten the mood. But she could see in his eyes that he was serious, that this was a subject he'd thought a lot about. Suddenly May panicked, scared that if they stood there any longer he might ask her to talk about things she just wasn't ready to share, memories she didn't want to revisit. 'Come on, let's go. They'll be closing in a minute. We don't want to get locked in.'

May started walking, her hurried steps scattering pebbles, leaving Ben gazing after her, wondering what on earth was going on.

'I can't do it Fay, I can't.' May sat at the desk in her room, twisting the phone cord between her fingers, gazing out of the window into a thick fog. 'I just can't.'

'Well,' Faith said, 'whether or not you've got what it takes isn't really the point right now, is it? The real question is: do you want to?'

May was silent for a moment. 'No. Yes. I don't know. I never did, before I met Ben. And now I just...'

'What?' Faith asked softly. 'You... what?'

'I feel... I feel...' May stumbled, almost too scared to put it into words. 'Sometimes I feel a completely overwhelming desire in my heart to do it. But then I think I'm just being mad, naïve, stupid...'

'Being a little hard on yourself at all?' Faith asked, a light tone in her voice.

May giggled. 'I suppose so. But I just... I really, really don't want to mess up. Not that. I mean, I figure if I mess up my own life, in the end the only person I really hurt is me, but with a kid –'

'And Ben,' Faith said, 'and of course everyone else who loves you.'

'Well yes, true,' May admitted. 'But, I mean, even if Ben and I split up he'd be okay, he'd move on and all that. But with a kid… you mess that up and they don't get over it; it wounds them forever.'

'Says who?' Faith asked.

'Well, everyone knows that,' May said. 'I mean, if your parents mess up, then they mess you up forever. They bequeath you loads of… "baggage"; you carry it for the rest of your life, and you have to spend loads of time learning how to let it go. And I don't want to do that. I don't want to be responsible for permanently messing up somebody else's life.'

Thinking she'd made the definitive point, May looked out of the window again and wondered if the fog would clear, squinting through it, trying to see the bridge.

'You know,' Faith said, 'I don't think this is about fear. I think it's about forgiveness.'

May was silent for a moment. 'What?'

'I don't think this is *just* about you being scared of being a bad parent,' Faith said. 'It's about you still blaming your parents for all the issues you've ever had: low self-esteem, lack of courage, all that stuff…'

'No,' May said firmly. 'No, that's not true, I don't, I don't –'

Faith stopped her. 'Hey, remember what you told me about living in denial? Well, perhaps if you don't say "no" so quickly, and give yourself a moment, you might realise I have a point. Perhaps, possibly, maybe…'

'Sorry,' May said softly. 'Yes, I suppose you might, just possibly, have a point.'

'Good!' Faith clapped. 'I thought so.'

'How did you know?'

'Deduction. Supreme intelligence. Intuition. Your cousin is not to be trifled with, you know.'

'Yes, I'm starting to see that.' May smiled.

'The thing is,' Faith explained, 'if you blame your parents, especially your father, for giving you "issues" that messed you up, then you'll blame yourself for whatever happens to your kids, whether or not it has anything to do with you.'

May squeezed her eyes shut and bit her lip.

'But you have to remember,' Faith went on, 'your life is *your* life, and it's up to you to make the most of it, right now. It doesn't matter what happened in the past. You'll never get anywhere by looking back and blaming. Your parents did the best they could, just like you always do, and of course they made mistakes; they messed up, just like we all do. But if you blame them, or indeed you, for everything that's gone "wrong", then no matter how good life finally gets you'll never let yourself enjoy it. You'll have to suffer, just to justify the blame.'

May was silent, letting it all sink in. She opened her eyes again and looked out at the fog, relieved that Faith was at the other end of a phone in England

and not able to see her face. Because, while May still didn't want to admit it, she knew her cousin was right.

'Yes,' May said at last. 'Okay, so you have a point. My whole fairy-tale fantasy about perfect parenthood, the ideal I couldn't live up to, has come from blaming my own parents, my father, for not doing it right, for everything that went wrong.'

'Ah, but that's another thing I have a theory about,' Faith said, 'and it works extremely well, whether or not it's really true.'

May raised an eyebrow, wondering what wacky theory her kooky cousin had concocted to see her through life's traumas. Although May had to admit, given how happy Faith always seemed to be, whatever it was, it certainly worked.

'I have this theory, about the wisdom of the heart, or the soul, I'm not really sure which,' Faith said, 'but the point is that it's our highest wisdom, and it brings all events into our lives for us to learn everything we need to learn in order to be truly happy, like letting go, loving ourselves, surrendering, peace, compassion, empathy… any number of things. Anyway, it means to me that painful events, although momentarily heartbreaking, aren't ultimately awful. At least they don't have to be. Because, if we really want to, we can use them to make us more compassionate, kind, thoughtful, understanding… So, while they begin as heartbreaks, they can end as gifts.'

May sighed. 'Well, I like the theory, but I can't see how something like my dad leaving me could be a gift. Of course my life would have been better if it hadn't happened. And the same can be said of anything awful' – May paused to think of some awful things – 'like death, divorce, any kind of devastation. I don't think…'

'Yes, of course,' Faith said, 'if you choose to see it and live with it like that, then you're right. But the point is it's really up to you. You can turn it into a gift; you can let the event either open your heart more or shut it down. Which, of course, you'd be perfectly within your rights to do, but it would mean you'd never be happy again.'

'It's not that easy though,' May objected. 'If you're angry and hurt, you can't just decide not to be.'

'Oh, but you can,' Faith replied. 'That's the first step. You can decide to begin to forgive your father, and you can begin to forgive yourself. You can decide to stop fighting reality, to let go of fairy tales and to start to surrender to the fact that we're all flawed and we're all in need of forgiveness. You can accept that life is both totally messed up and yet extraordinarily beautiful. Or you can keep on insisting that it should be different, more peaceful and less painful. But I'm afraid it is what it is, and it's up to you to make the best of it.'

May smiled. 'I feel like a little kid, who's just been given a good talking to by her teacher.'

'Well,' Faith said, giggling, 'that's because it's time to realise that sometimes life is sweet, and sometimes it isn't, but refusing to forgive your dad will only make it sourer and mean that you won't give yourself the gift of having a child, even if you really want one.'

May couldn't help but smile at Faith's persuasive logic. 'Yes, nice segue, oh crazy but brilliant cousin of mine.'

'Right. Good, then stop worrying that everything will go wrong, 'cause even if it does, it doesn't really,' Faith said. 'Have a baby, write a book, do whatever you want.'

May wished her cousin was there so she could give her a huge hug. 'You are amazing,' she said instead.

'Oh, I know,' Faith said lightly, 'I know.'

For the rest of the day May sat at her desk, tapping her fingers on the wood, chewing the end of her pen, occasionally scribbling things down and then crossing them out. Five hours later the fog had cleared, the sun was starting to set behind the Golden Gate Bridge and May had a full, unblemished paragraph.

'A little messy and a little perfect,' she said, after reading it through for the tenth time. 'A great place to start.'

Doughnut jumped onto the desk and sat down on the page, his furry bum covering every word. May laughed and lifted him off.

'I suppose having a child would be a bit like having a hundred cats, in which case I'd better postpone it for a while, or finish this book before she or he is born.'

She held Doughnut in her arms and walked slowly down the spiral staircase, recalling what Faith had said. It occurred to her that her cousin's wisdom could help create an interesting book, and she began thinking about how she could structure it. As she did so, May crossed the flat and descended the main staircase to see Ben, since she now had something rather important to say.

'Are you sure?' Ben asked for the twentieth time as they lay in bed together. He had one hand on her belly and was gazing at her intently, his big brown eyes wide with hope. 'Are you *really* sure?'

'No,' May said with a small smile, 'and since I can never know how this'll all turn out I don't think I ever will be. But I do know that I love you, that I feel the desire to do this deep in my heart, and that I'm ready for another…'

'Crazy adventure?'

'Yes,' May replied, grinning. 'exactly.'

It didn't happen that month, or the next, or the sixth month after that. They kept trying, and May kept writing, and by the spring she had a new book. She showed it to Ben first, who loved it and kept promising he wasn't biased. And May believed him, since they had so far kept their agreement of compassionate honesty, no matter what. And now she wanted to show it to someone else – to Lily.

May had seen Lily every week since her return. They had dinner, with Megan and Ben, and saw each other at book readings and the like. May's agent still arranged various public-speaking engagements and other publicity events, and May went along with them as long as they were in good taste. She reinstated her own evenings of fun and inspiration, twice a week, talking to readers about their own men, money and chocolate challenges, and she tried her best to help. And, wherever she went, Ben was always in the front row.

This time May invited Lily for coffee and cake at The Tea Cup. May was early and stood chatting with Alice while she waited. A few months earlier she and Alice had founded the Insight & Inspiration Book Club and they spent many happy hours together trying out cake recipes and new books for the meetings.

'Hi.' Lily tapped May on the shoulder.

'Hey,' May said, turning round to hug her.

They bought cappuccinos and slices of caramel cake, and sat in the window, though this time Lily took the lucky chair.

'Apparently that chair has witnessed many marriage proposals,' May said, taking a sip of coffee and a big bite of cake.

'Oh yeah.' Lily smiled. 'That's lovely, but I bet none of them were as utterly fabulous as mine.'

'Really?' May asked, intrigued.

'Oh, absolutely,' Lily said. 'I asked Megan to marry me in our garden, at twilight, with a thousand fairy lights hanging through the trees. Of course, until they change the law, we can't actually get married. But since we've been unmarried for the last twenty-two years, I don't suppose a few more will make much difference.'

'You asked her?'

'Yes, why? D'you want tips?' Lily asked. 'Is that why we're here?'

'No,' May said, blushing. 'I wrote a new book, I'd love you to read it.'

Lily's eyes lit up. 'Now that is fabulous. I'd love to.'

May reached down and took the manuscript out of her bag and slid it across the table. Lily picked up the pages and read the title.

'*Happier Than She's Ever Been...*' Lily smiled. 'I don't suppose this would be another work of fiction based rather closely on fact, would it?'

'Well, yes,' May admitted. 'Yes, it might just be.'

'Wonderful.' Lily slipped it into her bag. 'Well then, I look forward to learning even more about you.'

'Me, and my cousin, and Ben, and you...'

'Me?' Lily looked surprised.

'Yep, I've added some of your wisdom in there,' May explained. 'I hope you don't mind. I can always change it, if you do.'

'Mind? Why should I mind? I'm flattered. Now I'll look forward to reading it even more.' Lily smiled and, just for a moment, May felt as though her mum was there, sitting at the table and smiling.

'What's the surprise?' Ben asked, as May led him through the gates of the Japanese Tea Garden.

'It wouldn't be one if I told you now, would it?' May said, taking him over the bridge and towards the bench where they had first sat together, three years earlier.

'Is it a good one?'

'Yes, I think so.'

They reached the bench. Ben sat down, looking up expectantly. 'Well?'

'Patience isn't one of your virtues, is it?' May smiled.

'Nope. So what is it?'

'Well' – May started to kneel on the pebbled path –

'it's not something to tell you; it's something to ask you.'

Ben started to smile.

'So here goes.' May became serious. 'Ben, will you
—'

'Yes. Yes. Yes.'

'Hey, I haven't even asked you yet!'

'Sorry, *bichana*, I couldn't wait. The suspense was killing me.'

'Oh, come on...'

'Okay, that's a lie,' Ben admitted. 'But I didn't want *you* to ask, I mean, of course I did, but *I* wanted to ask *you*.'

'Oh.' May smiled. 'I see.'

Ben shifted from the bench to the path and knelt in front of May, who was still kneeling herself. May giggled as a few passersby slowed to watch them. Ben put a finger to her lips.

'May, will you –'

'Yes,' she said. And they both laughed.

They walked all the way home, hand in hand, underneath a fogless sky spotted with stars. Then they had dinner, went to bed and made love. And that was the night it happened.

Three nights later May woke up sweating, her heart racing. This time she didn't try to calm herself down, or suppress her feelings and keep all her fears secret. Instead she woke Ben, who squinted up at her with a sleepy smile.

'I just had another dream,' May said. 'A portentous one.'

'Is that a word?' Ben mumbled.

'Yes, it's a word, of course it's a word. Well, at least I think it is,' May said. 'Anyway, that's not the point.'

'What is the point then, *bichana*?' Ben groaned. 'Is it specifically a three thirty a.m. point or one that could be made at nine a.m.?'

'I just met our son.' May couldn't help but smile. 'Well, his spirit at least.'

'Really?' Ben asked, his eyes shining. 'Really?'

May nodded. 'Yep, I think so, if my latent, and completely untested, psychic powers are anything to go by. And he told me something.'

'Oh?'

'He told me that this next adventure is going to be a brilliant and very bumpy ride.'

'Oh boy.' Ben laughed, pulling May into a hug. He held her tightly for a while, tucking his head into her shoulder, then wiped his eyes and looked into hers. 'Are you nervous?'

'Oh, no.' May smiled at him. 'Only vaguely terrified. But I have a little feeling that as long as my heart keeps beating, and I keep breathing, then it'll be all right. No matter how much I mess up, he'll be okay, and we'll be okay and, whatever goes wrong,' she said, thinking back to her conversation with Faith, 'death, divorce or devastation, if we keep looking for the good stuff in it all, then it'll work out. And, either way, life won't stop being –'

'Messy and beautiful and –'

'Perfect –'

'Exactly as it is –' Ben said.

'Right.' May smiled.

And then they kissed.

www.menmoneyandchocolate.com

If you've enjoyed May's experience of enlightenment, and want to have a magical life too, then we invite you to seek inspiration from the real-life Rose: Vicky van Praag

vicky@vickyvanpraag.co.uk

She'll give you all the insight and inspiration you need to make all your daydreams come true: a loving relationship, work that fills your heart, and a body that makes you smile!

Visit our brilliant blog – full of inspiration, chocolate and other sweet things. And find us on Facebook for updates, giveaways and lots more!

ABOUT THE AUTHOR

Menna van Praag is the author of the bestselling *Men, Money & Chocolate*, the autobiographical tale of a woman who longs to be a writer but lacks the courage and self-belief to succeed. As a little girl, long before self-doubt settled in, Menna wrote stories and read them aloud to anyone who would listen. As a teenager, her English Literature teacher suggested her writing was 'publishable', thus planting a secret seed of hope in her heart. But, being full of self-doubt, Menna decided to focus on a sensible and safe future and went to Oxford University to take a degree in Modern History. There she read many books (texts during the day, novels at night) and tried to forget about writing her own.

© Mark Ashworth

She graduated into an office job but, sensible as it was, it also made her feel slightly suicidal and Menna realised it was writing or nothing. So, for the next eight years she worked as a waitress and wrote numerous unpublished novels. About to turn 30, with enough rejections to wallpaper her flat, she thought it might be time to give up hope. Luckily, a month before the birthday, Menna attended an enlightening workshop in New York, with Ariel & Shya Kane. Now determined never to give up, Menna remembered a life-changing conversation (one of many) with her mum, Vicky van Praag, and sat down to write a different book: about hope, courage, self-belief and truth.

Menna lives in Cambridge with her husband, Artur. *Happier Than She's Ever Been...* is her second (published) book. She is currently working on her third, *The House at the End of Hope Street*.